VALERIE O'MALLEY

The Scarlet Strangler

Detective Sam Ellis and Rachel Banks are in pursuit of a serial killer responsible for a series of murders in a small town.

"THE UITIMATE POSSESSION WAS, IN FACT, THE TALKING OF THE LIFE. AND THEN…. THE PHYSICAL POSSESSION OF THE REMAINS"

TED BUNDY

Contents

Chapter 1

A TOWN GRIPPED IN FEAR

The clock on the mantle chimed twelve, the sound echoing through the stillness of the night. Outside, the rain tapped a steady rhythm against the windows, creating a barrier between the warm, yellow glow of the living room and the dark world beyond.

In the quiet town of Willow Creek, the only noise was the occasional bark of a distant dog, punctuating the silence like an exclamation point. Detective Sam Ellis sat inside the house in his favorite chair, a half-empty mug of coffee cooling on the side table. He stared at the board in front of him, filled with newspaper clippings, notes, and photos connected by a web of red yarn. The unsolved case of the "Scarlet Strangler" had haunted the town for months, leaving a trail of fear and suspicion in its wake.

The Strangler's MO was as gruesome as it was baffling—always striking on rainy nights, leaving no fingerprints or DNA behind, and always leaving a peculiar calling card with each of their victims: a single, crimson ribbon. Sam had reviewed the evidence countless times, but the pieces never fit together. Each clue led to a dead end, and the killer remained elusive, taunting the town with their cleverness.

The phone on the desk rang shrilly, jolting Sam out of his thoughts. He picked it up, expecting to hear the voice of his partner, Rachel, with an update or a lead, but instead, it was the trembling voice of Mrs Clark, the elderly lady who lived two houses down. "Detective, I saw something," she whispered, the fear palpable through the receiver. "A figure, lurking in the shadows, they had… they had the ribbon."

Sam's heart raced. Could this be it? Could this be the break they needed? He assured Mrs. Clark that he'd be right over, hung up, and grabbed his raincoat, the adrenaline already coursing through his veins. Raindrops splashed against the pavement as he sprinted through the deserted streets, his flashlight casting eerie shadows along the sidewalks. As he approached her house, he noticed a dim light flickering in the window and the sound of a TV playing too loudly.

Mrs. Clark was shaking when she opened the door, her eyes wide with terror. She clutched her cardigan tightly, her knuckles white with tension. "It was just there," she pointed to the gap between her Neighbor's hedges, her eyes wide with terror. "I saw them place the ribbon on the fence post before they vanished."

Sam nodded, his mind racing. This was the closest they'd ever come to catching the Scarlet Strangler. He stepped into the rain, eyes scanning the area as he approached the ribbon. It fluttered in the breeze, a stark crimson against the dark wood. He took a deep breath, steeling himself for what he might find.

As he reached for the ribbon, his hand hovered for a moment. It was wet, but not entirely from the rain. There was a sticky residue that made him wince. Carefully, he placed it in an evidence bag, sealing it with trembling hands. He radioed Rachel, his voice low and urgent. "I've got something. Meet me at Mrs Clarks'".

The wind picked up, sending chills down Sam's spine. The rain grew heavier, soaking his coat and plastering his hair on his forehead. He felt a strange sense of déjà vu as if he'd walked these streets a hundred times before, chasing shadows that always slipped away. But this time was different. The ribbon was actual, a tangible connection to the killer.

Chapter 2

W HISPERS OF THE SCARLET STRANGER

Rachel's voice crackled through the radio, confirming her arrival. Sam waited impatiently, his eyes never leaving the ribbon. The TV's flickering light cast a strobe-like pattern across the wet pavement, painting the scene in an unsettling rhythm. He heard the distant wail of the siren, growing closer with each pulse, cutting through the quiet of the night like a knife.

When Rachel arrived, she looked at the ribbon, and her eyes narrowed. She knew the significance of this discovery. "We can't let this lead go cold," she said, her voice determined. Together, they searched the area, each step careful not to disturb the delicate balance of potential evidence. The rain had washed away any footprints, but the ribbon was a beacon of hope in the sea of despair that had become Willow Creek.

The siren grew louder, the patrol car's flashing lights piercing the darkness. Rachel gave Sam a knowing glance, and they both knew that the quiet town's tranquility was about to be shattered once again. The car pulled up, and two officers jumped out, their faces a mix of dread and anticipation. Sam filled them in quickly, handing them the evidence bag. "Keep this safe," he instructed, his voice firm.

The officers nodded, retreating to their vehicle to log the new evidence. Rachel turned to Sam, her eyes gleaming with determination. "We need to move fast before the trail goes cold." They decided to split up, Rachel taking the left side of the street to canvass the Neighborhood for any information while Sam took the right. Each house they approached had its own story etched into its facade, but tonight, all of Willow Creek was a potential crime scene.

The rain had grown into a storm now, the wind howling through the streets, making it difficult to hear over the din of nature. Sam knocked on the first door, the sound muffled by the rain. A sleepy man in a bathrobe answered, rubbing his eyes. Sam flashed his badge and quickly explained the situation. The man's expression shifted from irritation to fear. He hadn't seen anything, he claimed, but the tremor in his voice suggested he was hiding something.

As Rachel moved from house to house, she found more of the same—frightened faces and tightly shut doors. Yet, she could feel the collective sigh of relief from the townspeople, knowing that the police were actively hunting the Scarlet Strangler. Despite the cold, Rachel felt a warmth spread through her chest, a sense of purpose that had been missing for too long in this stagnant case.

The storm grew more intense, lightning illuminating the night sky and casting eerie flashes across the town. Sam's gut told him they were getting closer. The ribbon felt like a breadcrumb left by the killer, a taunt or perhaps a clue to their identity. His thoughts were interrupted by a sudden sound—a muffled scream carried on the wind. His heart skipped a beat, and he sprinted towards the source.

As he rounded the corner, he saw a figure bolting from a side alley and disappearing into the rain. Without hesitation, Sam took off in pursuit, his boots splashing through puddles and the rain stinging his face. The figure was fast, weaving through the narrow streets, but Sam was relentless. The chase led them deeper into the heart of Willow Creek, where the houses grew farther apart, and the trees loomed like silent sentinels.

Chapter 3

DEADLY GAME

The scream grew louder, and Sam's heart hammered in his chest. He knew he was close. The figure darted down another alley, and Sam followed, his flashlight bobbing wildly. The alley opened into a small clearing, and in the flickering light of a lone streetlamp, he saw it—another ribbon, lying in a pool of rainwater, a crimson ribbon just like before.

The figure darted into a narrow alleyway, and Sam followed, his flashlight bobbing in the dark. His eyes adjusted to the gloom, and he caught a glimpse of a red blur—the ribbon tied around the attacker's wrist like a grim trophy. The alley opened into a small park; the swings slid ghostly in the lightning strobe. The figure leaped over a bench and vanished into the trees beyond.

Sam's instincts took over, his legs pumping as he crashed through the underbrush. The storm had turned the park into a treacherous obstacle course, but he pushed on, driven by the knowledge that the Strangler could be just meters ahead. Rachel's voice grew louder in his ear, guiding him from her position on the other side of the park.

The rain was a torrent now, soaking him to the bone, but he barely noticed. His eyes were locked on the crimson flicker that seemed to dance just out of reach. The sound of the killer's footsteps grew more evident, the squelch of wet earth beneath their boots. Sam's heart hammered in his chest, a drumbeat keeping time with the thunder above.

The alley opened into a small, dimly lit park. The playground swings swayed in the wind, the metal chains clinking mournfully. Rachel's voice grew more explicit in his ear, urging him on. The figure was close—too close for comfort.

Sam's boots splashed through puddles as he pursued the crimson blur. His eyes darted around, searching for any sign of movement in the storm. The lightning flashed, revealing a shadowy figure climbing over a picnic table, the ribbon tied around their wrist fluttering like a macabre flag. Rachel's voice grew more urgent. "Sam, I'm coming around the north side of the park. Be careful!"

The figure slipped into the dense trees, their footsteps growing fainter. Sam's pulse raced, the adrenaline thrumming through his veins like a baseline. The rain stung his eyes, but he didn't dare slow down. This was his chance to bring the Scarlet Strangler to justice finally.

The park's lights flickered in the storm, casting an eerie glow on the slick grass. Sam's flashlight beam bobbed and weaved as he sprinted through the maze of trunks and underbrush. Thunder cracked overhead, and the world was bathed in white light for a moment, revealing the killer just ahead. The ribbon was a stark contrast against the dark fabric of their clothing.

The figure darted behind a large oak, and Sam followed, his breathing ragged. His hand hovered over his gun, its weight comforting in his holster. As he rounded the tree, the killer was nowhere to be seen. He paused, listening intently, his senses in high alert. Rainwater dripped from the leaves above, mingling with the scent of fresh earth and something else—a faint metallic tinge that sent a shiver down his spine.

A sudden rustle from the bushes made him whirl around, his flashlight cutting through the darkness. There was a brief glimpse of red, and then—silence. Sam's heart was a jackhammer in his chest as he approached the bushes, his hand tightening on his gun grip. The storm had become a cacophony of sounds, making it difficult to pinpoint the killer's location.

The bushes parted with a crackling of branches, and a figure emerged, drenched and desperate. It was a woman, her eyes wild with fear. The crimson ribbon was tied around her neck, not her wrist, starkly contrasting her pale skin. She stumbled backward, her hands up in surrender. "Please, don't shoot," she begged, her voice trembling.

Sam's instincts screamed at him to capture her, but his mind raced. This wasn't the Scarlet Strangler—the build was wrong, and the movements were too erratic. "Who are you?" he demanded, his gun still trained on her. She gasped for breath, her eyes darting from side to side as if searching for an escape.

"I... I'm a victim," she stuttered, her voice barely audible over the storm. She fumbled with the ribbon, her trembling fingers struggling to untie the knot. "They left me here; said I was next if I didn't do as they said."

Sam's grip on his gun loosened slightly, his mind racing. The killer could be watching them, using her as bait. He holstered his weapon and stepped closer, his eyes never leaving hers. "Come with me," he instructed firmly. "We'll get you somewhere safe and figure this out."

The woman's relief was palpable as she nodded, her teeth chattering from the cold and fear. Together, they sprinted back towards the lights of the town, the rain hammering down on them. Rachel's voice was constant in Sam's ear, guiding them to a nearby safe house they'd set up for such a situation.

Chapter 4

THE VICTIMS VOICE

Once inside, they stripped off their soaked clothes, the woman's trembling hands struggling with the sodden fabric. Sam offered her a blanket, his eyes never leaving her face as she recounted her harrowing tale. Her name was Laura, a local artist who had been walking her dog when the Strangler grabbed her. He'd left her with the ribbon, a chilling warning of what would come.

The room was small and sparse, but it felt like a fortress compared to the wild night outside. Rachel arrived, her clothes drenched, her eyes filled with concern. Laura's story was consistent with the Strangler's MO, but the lack of physical evidence made them all feel like they were grasping at straws. Rachel took her statement, her pen flying across the page as the storm raged.

As Laura spoke, Sam couldn't shake the feeling that something was off. Her story was too pat, too convenient. He excused himself, stepping into the hallway to call for backup. His eyes scanned the room as he talked into the radio, noticing the rainwater tracking mud across the floor. Something didn't add up.

When he returned, Rachel was finishing up with Laura. The woman looked up at him with a mix of hope and terror. He knew they needed to move quickly. If the Strangler had sent her as a decoy, they were close. Rachel nodded, understanding the gravity of the situation.

"We're going to get you to the station," Sam told Laura, his voice firm. "You'll be safe there."

Her eyes searched his for reassurance, and he gave a small, comforting smile. Rachel handed her a cup of hot tea, and Laura clutched it like a lifeline, her hands still trembling. Sam noticed that her nails were ragged, bitten down to the quick, a stark contrast to the meticulously painted fingers he'd seen in her artwork around town.

The patrol car pulled up, its lights stroking through the windows, casting a frantic pattern on the walls. Laura's eyes widened, and Rachel took her hand, leading her into the storm. Sam followed closely, his eyes scanning the shadows. As they reached the car, Rachel opened the door, and Laura slipped inside, the warmth from the heated seats enveloping her like a blanket.

Sam climbed in the back, his eyes never leaving Laura's reflection in the rearview mirror. Rachel slammed the door shut and called for backup on the radio. The car lurched forward, tires splashing through puddles as they raced towards the station. Laura sat shaking, her eyes darting between the two detectives.

The station was a beacon in the storm, the neon lights of the sign flickering in the downpour. The car screeched to a halt outside, and Rachel opened the door, helping Laura out. The warmth from the building spilled onto the sidewalk, and Rachel could feel the tension in the air as they hurried inside.

In the interrogation room, Laura's story began to unravel. Rachel noticed the inconsistencies, the way Laura's eyes darted around the room, avoiding their gazes. The ribbon around her neck was the only thing that seemed genuine. "Why don't you tell us what happened?"

Rachel asked gently, her voice a stark contrast to the storm outside.

Chapter 5

T HE PLOT THICKENS

Laura took a deep, shuddering breath, her eyes welling with tears. She admitted that she had found the ribbon near the park, her curiosity piqued by the dreadful rumors swirling around town. She'd been too scared to come forward, fearing she might become the Strangler's next target. Sam leaned in, his instincts screaming that there was more to her story.

"You didn't see the killer?" he pressed, his voice low and measured. Laura's gaze dropped to her trembling hands; the mug of tea was now forgotten. "Not at first," she whispered. "But when I tried to leave,… they grabbed me." Rachel's pen paused mid-stroke, her eyes narrowing.

"Who grabbed you?" Rachel's voice was calm, but her grip on the pen was tight. Laura swallowed hard, her eyes flicking from Rachel to Sam again. "I don't know," she admitted. "They were wearing a hood, and their voice was muffled."

The room was silent, save for the rain drumming against the windows. Sam's mind raced, trying to piece together the puzzle before them. Rachel leaned in, her eyes searching Laura's face. "But you saw something, didn't you?"

Laura's shoulders slumped. "A glimpse of an eye," she murmured. "It was… cold, like ice." Sam felt a chill run down his spine. Rachel's gaze sharpened. "What color was the eye?"

"I don't know," Laura said, her voice cracking. "The light was strange—like it was glowing." Rachel and Sam exchanged a look. This was new information, something they hadn't anticipated. Rachel jotted down notes, her brow furrowed. "Was there anything else? Anything that stood out?"

Laura took a deep breath, visibly gathering her thoughts. "Their hand," she whispered. "It was… covered in tattoos." Rachel and Sam's eyes met again, a silent acknowledgment passing between them. The Scarlet Strangler had never left a tattooed handprint at any crime scene. Was Laura telling the truth, or was she part of the game?

The interrogation continued into the early morning hours, the storm outside mirroring the tumultuous questions within the small, stark room. Laura's story remained consistent, yet the nagging doubt remained. Rachel stepped out to make a call, leaving Sam alone with Laura. He studied her, the artist's slender hands wrapped tightly around the mug, the ribbon still tied around her neck—a grim reminder of the horror she'd escaped.

When Rachel returned, she looked grim. "No reports of anyone matching Laura's description being in the area during the storm," she informed Sam. "And no new crime scenes." Laura's eyes filled with relief, but Sam's mind was racing. Rachel nodded at him, and he knew she was thinking the same thing.

They decided to take Laura home under strict surveillance. As they approached her house, the rain finally began to ease, revealing a quiet, sleeping town. Rachel pulled the car to a stop in front of Laura's house, the headlights casting a pool of light on the drenched sidewalk. Sam stepped out, his eyes scanning the darkness.

"You're sure there's no one here?" he asked, his hand resting on the gun. Laura nodded, her eyes wide with fear. "Yes." Rachel took her hand, offering a reassuring smile. "We'll be watching you," she promised. Laura stepped out of the car, the cold air wrapping around her. She looked up at her house, the windows dark and foreboding.

Chapter 6

A KILLER LURKS AMONG US

The detectives followed her to the door, their flashlights cutting through the misty air. Sam noticed a slight tremble in Laura's hand as she inserted her key into the lock. Rachel leaned in, her voice a whisper. "Remember, if anything happens, call us immediately." Laura nodded, her teeth chattering. "I will."

Inside, the house starkly contrasted with the night's chaos—warm, dry, and eerily silent. Laura turned on the lights, casting a soft glow through the hallway. The detectives scanned the area, searching for any signs of a break-in or a clue that the Scarlet Strangler had been there. The living room was undisturbed, the furniture arranged with a comforting familiarity. Rachel's eyes fell on a framed painting above the mantle, a ribbon of crimson snaking through the canvas. Laura noticed her gaze and flinched.

"It's just… I was working on it before," she mumbled, her voice trailing. Rachel nodded, making a mental note to question her about it later. For now, the priority was to ensure Laura's safety. They checked the locks and windows, advised her to leave the lights on, and promised to keep an eye on the house from their parked car.

As they stepped back outside, the rain had turned to a gentle patter, the storm finally beginning to wane. Rachel turned to Sam, her eyes reflecting the yellow glow of the streetlight. "We can't leave her alone," she said firmly. Sam nodded his hand on the car door. "I'll grab the night-vision goggles."

They set up a discreet surveillance post in the car, the engine humming softly to keep the heat in. Rachel's eyes never left Laura's house, watching the windows for any sign of movement. Sam scanned the street, his thoughts racing. The tattooed hand was an unexpected twist that didn't fit the Strangler's profile. Was Laura a victim or a clever accomplice?

Time she stretched thin, the seconds ticking away with the rhythm of the rain. Rachel's phone buzzed with an incoming message. She read it, her face tightening. "The lab results are in," she said, her voice low. "The ribbon's got DNA on it, but it's not in the system."

Sam's gaze snapped to her. "That means it could be our break," he murmured, his eyes never leaving Laura's house. Rachel nodded, her thoughts racing. "We need to get a sample from Laura to rule her out or in." The words hung heavy in the air, a stark reminder that their supposed victim could be holding the key to the case.

The night grew quiet, the storm retreating into the distance. Rachel's eyes burned with fatigue, but she knew they couldn't let their guard down. "We're getting closer," she said, more to herself than Sam. "I can feel it." He nodded, his eyes never straying from the house.

As the hours ticked by, Rachel's phone buzzed again. It was a message from one of the officers they'd left to canvass the neighborhood. "Got a hit on the ribbon," it read. We found a similar one in a dumpster two blocks from Mrs. Clark's. We're on it." Rachel's pulse quickened. The killer was taunting them, leaving breadcrumbs to follow.

The rain had ceased, leaving the world outside the car a soggy mess, the only sound the occasional drip from the leaves. Rachel stifled a yawn, her eyes still glued to Laura's house. The quiet was unnerving, a stark contrast to the tumultuous events of the evening. Sam's gaze flicked to the clock on the dashboard. It was almost dawn, and the promise of a new day was beginning to lighten the sky.

Chapter 7

THE KILLER'S NEXT MOVE

"We need to get some rest," Rachel murmured, her voice thick with exhaustion. "We can't do her any good if we fall asleep on the job." Sam nodded in agreement, his eyes finally leaving the house to meet hers. They'd been at this for hours, but the case felt more alive than ever.

They decided to take shifts, Rachel agreeing to stay awake while Sam slept for a few minutes. He leaned back in his seat, the leather cold and unforgiving, and closed his eyes, letting the rhythm of the rain outside lull him into a fitful doze. Rachel took over the watch, her eyes heavy but focused.

An hour later, Sam woke with a start, his dreams filled with images of the Scarlet Strangler slipping away into the night. Rachel was still staring out the window, her eyes unblinking. "Nothing?" he asked, his voice gruff from sleep. She shook her head, and they switched places.

As Rachel leaned back, her eyes closed almost immediately; Sam took up the vigil. His eyes scanned the silent street, the only movement the sway of wet branches in the breeze. The ribbon found in the dumpster played on his mind—was it a clue or a distraction?

His thoughts were interrupted by the sound of a door opening. Laura stepped out onto her porch, the light from the hallway casting a warm glow around her. She looked around nervously before locking the door, the ribbon still tied around her neck. Sam's hand tightened on the steering wheel. Why would she go outside after what she'd been through?

Rachel stirred in the passenger seat, her eyes snapping open. She took in the scene, her expression mirroring Sam's concern. Laura glanced up and down the street before going to the edge of her property. She paused, looking directly at the car. For a moment, Sam was sure she'd seen them. But she didn't react, just took a deep breath and turned back towards the house.

They watched her retreat into the warmth, the door clicking shut behind her. Rachel leaned forward, her eyes still on the house. "That was odd," she murmured. Sam nodded, his gut twisting. Something was off, and they both knew it.

Their unease grew as the night remained quiet, the only sound the occasional car passing by. Rachel's phone buzzed again, and she read the message with a frown. "The ribbon in the dumpster—it's definitely from the same source as the one Laura had." Sam's eyes narrowed. "So, the Strangler was watching us." Rachel nodded, the implication heavy.

They decided to keep their distance, not wanting to spook Laura or alert the killer to their suspicion. Rachel took the wheel, and they drove slowly through the deserted streets, their eyes peeled for any sign of movement. The sky began to lighten, the promise of dawn a pale glimmer on the horizon.

As they circled the block, Sam's phone buzzed. It was a text from the lab: the DNA on the ribbon was female. Rachel's knuckles whitened on the steering wheel. "We need to bring her in," she said, her voice tight. "Her story doesn't add up."

Chapter 8

A WEB OF LIES

They pulled outside the station, the early morning light revealing a tired town still afraid. Inside, the buzz of activity was a stark contrast to the quiet streets. Rachel and Sam quickly briefed their captain on Laura's inconsistencies and the DNA evidence. The captain nodded gravely. "Bring her in," he said. We'll sort this out."

They didn't bother to warn Laura—there was no time for gentle explanations. Rachel knocked firmly on the door, her eyes scanning the surrounding area for any signs of danger. Laura answered, her face a mask of confusion that quickly turned to fear. "What's happening?" she asked, her voice shaky.

Sam stepped forward, his badge glinting in the early light. "We need to talk," he said, his voice firm but not unkind. Laura's eyes darted between them; Rachel stepped aside, allowing Sam to lead Laura to the car. She was shivering, whether from the cold or fear, they couldn't tell.

The ride to the station was tense, Laura's eyes never leaving the road ahead. Rachel sat in the back, her hand resting on the handcuffs in her pocket. Sam's eyes were on Laura in the rearview mirror, his expression unreadable. They pulled into the station's underground garage, the fluorescent lights flickering to life as they descended. The space was empty, save for a few patrol cars and the sound of rain echoing off the concrete.

In the interrogation room, Laura's fear grew palpable. Rachel took a seat across from her, her eyes unwavering. "We need to talk about the ribbon," Rachel said, her voice steady. Laura's hand flew to her neck, her eyes wide. "What ribbon?" she asked, her voice quivering.

Sam slammed a bag onto the table, the crimson fabric spilling out. Laura gasped, her eyes filling with tears. "This one," he said, his voice tight. Rachel pulled out the evidence bag, the ribbon coiled inside like a serpent ready to strike. Laura's eyes darted to the door, calculating.

"Why did you lie to us?" Rachel's voice was calm, but her eyes were like ice. Laura's facade crumbled, her shoulders dropping. "I didn't mean to," she whispered. "They said if I didn't…" Rachel leaned in, her gaze unyielding. "Who said?" Laura's voice was barely audible. "The Strangler. They called me and said they knew about my art and liked it. They said I'd be next if I didn't do as they said."

Sam's hand slammed on the table, making Laura flinch. "What did they want you to do?" His eyes were dark with anger. Laura took a shaky breath. "They sent me the ribbon, told me to wear it, to make it look like I was one of the victims." Rachel's pen paused the silence in the room thick with tension. "And what did they say would happen if you didn't?"

"They said… they said they'd come for me," Laura's voice was a mere whisper. Rachel leaned in closer, her eyes searching Laura's. "But you didn't just wear it, did you?" Laura's gaze dropped to her lap, her hands fidgeting with the fabric of her dress. Rachel's voice was gentle, but her eyes were sharp. "You went to the park, didn't you? You knew we'd find you there."

Sam's jaw clenched, his mind racing. "What was your part in this?" He demanded. Laura's eyes snapped up, meeting his. "I didn't do anything," she insisted, her voice pitching. "They just… they just wanted me to scare you." Rachel's eyes narrowed. "Why?" Laura's voice trembled. "They said you were getting too close and had to be thrown off the scent."

The room grew colder, the truth of Laura's admission hanging in the air. Rachel leaned back in her chair, her gaze never leaving Laura's face. "We need to know everything," she said, her voice measured. "Everything you know about the Scarlet Strangler." Laura took a deep breath, her eyes darting around the room as if searching for an escape.

"They called me," she began, her voice shaking. "They said they admired my art, that it was… it was 'fitting' for their 'work.'" Rachel's stomach turned at the thought of someone using Laura's creativity to justify their crimes. "They sent me the ribbon, told me to put it on, and wait for you in the park."

"And the tattooed hand?" Sam's voice was low, his eyes boring into Laura's. She looked away, her cheeks flushing. "They said they'd leave their mark, that you'd know it was them." Rachel's mind raced. If Laura was telling the truth, the Scarlet Strangler was playing a much more twisted game than they'd imagined.

Laura spoke rapidly now, her words tumbling out in a rush. "They told me to say I saw an eye that was cold and glowing. They said it would throw you off." Rachel leaned in, her eyes searching Laura's. "What else did they tell you?" Laura's breath hitched. "They said… they said they'd leave me alone if I did this."

The room was silent except for the clock ticking on the wall. Rachel's gaze was unwavering, her mind racing. "But you don't believe them, do you?" Laura's eyes filled with tears. "No," she whispered. "I don't know what to believe anymore."

Rachel leaned forward, her voice gentle. "You're safe here, Laura. We'll protect you." Laura's shoulders heaved with relief, but her eyes remained haunted. Rachel knew that words of comfort wouldn't erase the terror she'd experienced.

Chapter 9

U NCOVERING THE CONNECTION

The interrogation room was a stark reminder of the gravity of their situation. The cold, sterile walls seemed to close around them as Laura recounted the chilling details of her encounter with the Scarlet Strangler. Rachel listened intently, her mind piecing together the puzzle of Laura's involvement. Was she indeed a victim, or was there more to her story?

"What did the voice on the phone sound like?" Rachel asked, her pen poised over her notebook. Laura's eyes grew distant as she recalled the memory. "It was… muffled, almost inhuman. Like they were using some device to disguise it." Sam leaned in, his eyes sharp. "Did they mention anything about the other victims?"

Laura's gaze dropped to the table, her voice barely audible. "They said… they knew where I lived, who my friends were. They knew everything about me." Rachel felt a chill run down her spine. The Scarlet Strangler had been watching Laura, orchestrating this whole encounter. "They threatened your loved ones?"

"No," Laura said, her voice cracking. "They just… knew. It was like they were inside my head." Rachel shared a concerned look with Sam. The killer's reach was more expansive than they'd thought. They had to find a way to end this before anyone else got hurt.

"What about the eye?" Sam pressed, his voice softer this time. Laura shuddered. "It was just a story they made me tell. I didn't see the Strangler's face." Rachel nodded, jotting down notes. Laura's eyes searched their faces, desperate for some reassurance.

The clock on the wall ticked away, each second a silent accusation. Rachel's mind raced, trying to connect the dots. Laura had been manipulated; that much was clear. But to what end? The Scarlet Strangler was clever, playing on her fears and using her as a pawn in their twisted game.

"What do you know about the tattoo?" Rachel's voice was firm, cutting through Laura's distress. Laura fidgeted with the ribbon, her eyes downcast. "Just that it was… significant. They said it was their signature." Rachel shared a look with Sam. This was a new lead, a clue they hadn't had before.

They decided to keep Laura in protective custody while they worked on tracing the call and finding the tattoo's significance. Laura was taken to a secure room, her eyes wide with fear and confusion. Rachel gave her a reassuring pat before closing the door, leaving her with the echo of their footsteps.

Back in the office, Rachel and Sam dived into their computers, searching for any known criminals with a tattooed hand. The database was vast, but they had to narrow it down. Rachel's fingers flew over the keyboard, searching for patterns, while Sam studied the few details Laura had provided. "Anything?" Rachel asked, hope lacing her voice.

Sam grunted, his eyes scanning through mugshots. "Not yet," he said, his frustration growing. "But we can't ignore that Laura's story has holes." Rachel nodded, her mind racing. "It's possible she's being manipulated, but it's also possible she's an accomplice." They had to consider every angle, no matter how unsettling.

Their conversation was interrupted by a knock on the door. It was one of the officers from the night shift, a young man named Jenkins. "Detectives," he said, his face serious. "We've got a new lead. A local tattoo artist came forward. Someone matching the Strangler's description said they got a crimson ribbon tattoo on their hand last week." Rachel's eyes lit up. "That's it," she murmured, her voice filled with excitement.

Chapter 10

THE NEW LEAD

They rushed to the tattoo parlor, the rain a distant memory as the sun began to rise. The artist, a burly man named Mike, was waiting for them, a nervous look etched on his face. "I don't know if it's related," he began, his hands shaking slightly. "But the guy was weird, real secretive." He described the tattoo in detail, the crimson ribbon wrapped around the base of the thumb, the color vivid and stark against the killer's pale skin.

Rachel's pulse quickened. This was the break they needed. "Do you have any security footage?" she asked, her voice tight with anticipation. Mike nodded, leading them to a back room filled with the faint scent of antiseptic and ink. He pulled out a small USB drive, handing it over with trembling hands. "It's all here," he said. "But be warned, he wore a hoodie so that you won't get a good look at his face."

They returned to the station, the USB stick feeling like a hot coal in Rachel's hand. The tension in the air was palpable as they uploaded the footage to the computer. Sam leaned in, his eyes scanning the grainy images. Rachel's heart skipped a beat as a figure in a hoodie entered the frame, their hand outstretched for the camera.

The tattoo was unmistakable—a crimson ribbon identical to the one on Laura's neck. The hand was male, the skin pale and devoid of other identifying marks. The figure was careful not to show their face, but the tattoo was straightforward. "We need to get this to forensics," Sam said, his voice tight. Rachel nodded, her eyes glued to the screen.

They handed over the footage and waited, the tension in the air thick. Laura's story had taken a dark turn, and Rachel couldn't shake the feeling that they were missing something. "Why would the Strangler use her?" Rachel mused, her eyes scanning the notes scattered on their desk. "What does he gain from this?"

Sam leaned back in his chair, rubbing his eyes. "Could be a diversion," he said. "Maybe they wanted us to focus on Laura while they struck again." Rachel nodded, the thought chilling her. The Scarlet Strangler had been elusive, leaving no apparent motive or pattern behind. This was a twist they hadn't anticipated.

The forensic team was already on it, analyzing the footage for any trace of the killer's identity. Rachel's phone buzzed with an incoming text from the lab. "They've found something," she said, her heart racing as she read the message. "The ribbon in Laura's house—it's not the same fabric as the one from the crime scenes."

Sam's eyebrows shot up. "What does that mean?" Rachel looked up from her phone, her eyes meeting his. "It means Laura's ribbon is a copy. The Strangler gave it to her." The implications were staggering. Laura was more than just a pawn; she was a decoy, a way to keep the cops guessing.

They decided to question Laura again, this time in a more accusatory tone. Rachel led the way into the interrogation room, her stride purposeful. Laura looked up from her chair, her eyes wide with fear. "What's going on?" she asked, her voice trembling. Rachel slammed the door behind her, the sound echoing in the small space.

"The ribbon," Rachel said, her voice hard. "It's a fake." Laura's eyes darted around the room, searching for an escape that wasn't there. "What do you mean?" she asked, her voice barely above a whisper. Sam stepped forward, his face a mask of anger. "You've been playing us," he said, his voice low and dangerous.

Laura's facade crumbled, and she broke into sobs. "They made me," she choked out. "They said they'd kill me if I didn't." Rachel leaned against the table, her arms crossed. "Who made you?" Laura looked up, her eyes pleading. "I don't know their name. They just… called me. They said they knew everything about me, my art, and the ribbon."

Rachel's gaze sharpened. "What ribbon?" Laura sniffled. "The one in the park. They said it was a message, a warning. They made me wear it." Rachel and Sam exchanged a look. Laura was either a master manipulator or a terrified victim. Rachel chose to believe the latter, for now.

"Alright, Laura," Rachel said, her voice softer. "Tell us everything you know. Every detail." Laura took a deep, shuddering breath. "They called me a few days ago and said they liked my paintings. They talked about the ribbon and how it symbolized something to them. They sent me one and told me to wear it in the park." Rachel leaned in; her eyes bored Laura's. "And what did they say would happen if you didn't?" Laura's voice dropped to a whisper. "They said they'd come for me."

Sam's jaw tightened. "But you didn't just wear it. You had to make it look like you were in trouble." Laura nodded, her eyes brimming with tears. "They said you'd find me, that it would throw you off their trail. That it would give them more time." Rachel felt a flicker of anger. Time for what? To kill again?

They pressed Laura for more information, but she claimed she had none. Rachel could see the fear in her eyes, and she believed Laura was telling the truth—or at least her version of it. The Scarlet Strangler was playing a dangerous game, using Laura as bait to evade capture. They had to find the killer before they claimed another victim.

Chapter 11

S USPECT AND SUSPICION

With Laura secured in a safe room, Rachel and Sam huddled in their office, discussing their next move. The fake ribbon was a clue, but to what? Rachel suggested they go through Laura's artwork, looking for connections to the ribbon motif or the Scarlet Strangler's MO. Sam agreed, and they headed to Laura's house, now a crime scene, with a new sense of urgency.

The place looked identical to the first visit, but something felt off. It looked staged; the scene was painted with a fine brush to mimic a painting. Rachel felt a knot form in her stomach as she entered the scene. Laura's art studio was at the back of the house, filled with vibrant canvases and the smell of paint. In the center of the room, a single crimson ribbon lay on the floor, starkly contrasting the colorful mess around it.

They searched Laura's art for patterns and clues. Rachel's eyes fell on a painting in the corner, hidden by a pile of discarded brushes. It was a portrait of a woman, her neck adorned with a crimson ribbon, her eyes wide with terror. Rachel's hand flew to her mouth. "Sam," she whispered, her voice trembling.

Sam joined her, his eyes scanning the painting. "It's Mrs. Jenkins," he said, his voice low. Rachel nodded, her heart racing. Laura had painted Mrs. Jenkins before her murder. "This means she's seen the Strangler," Rachel murmured. "Or was told to paint this."

They gathered Laura's artwork, the weight of their discovery pressing down on them like a storm cloud. They spread the paintings at the station across the conference room table. The crimson ribbon was a haunting motif that wove through her work, a macabre thread connecting each piece. Rachel's eyes searched the images, looking for patterns, for a face hidden in the brushstrokes.

"This is insane," Sam murmured, his voice hollow. "How could she not know?" Rachel didn't answer, her mind racing. The Scarlet Strangler had been taunting them through Laura's art, leaving breadcrumbs that led to dead ends. Each painting was a puzzle piece that, when put together, formed a disturbing picture of their elusive killer's mind.

They called in a forensic art analyst to examine Laura's work. Dr. Garcia, a sharp-eyed woman with a no-nonsense attitude, studied the paintings closely. "There's something off about these," she said, her eyes narrowing. "Look at the brushstrokes around the ribbon. It's not her usual style." Rachel leaned in, her gaze following Dr. Garcia's finger as it traced the ribbon's edge.

The strokes were harsher and more deliberate than the rest of Laura's art. It was as if someone else had painted the ribbon, inserting their twisted narrative into her work. Rachel felt a chill run down her spine. The Scarlet Strangler had not only been watching Laura but had also been influencing her art. "Could the killer have painted these?" she asked, her voice barely above a whisper.

Dr. Garcia pursed her lips, her eyes never leaving the canvas. "It's possible," she said, her voice measured. "But we'd need more evidence to be sure." Rachel nodded, her mind racing. Laura had been living under the killer's shadow, her life and art intertwined with their sick game. They had to find the connection before it was too late.

"What about the tattoo?" Rachel asked, her thoughts spinning. "Could it be a symbol that ties the victims together?" Dr. Garcia considered the question. "It's a significant detail," she said, eyes scanning the room. "But without more context, it's difficult to say for certain."

Rachel and Sam exchanged a look. They had to dig deeper. They decided to re-interview Laura, this time with a more focused line of questioning. As they approached the interrogation room, Rachel felt a sense of dread. Laura's story had been consistent, but Rachel couldn't shake the feeling that there was more to it.

Inside, Laura sat in the same chair, looking paler and more drawn than before. Rachel sat opposite her, eyes searching Laura's face for any sign of deceit. "Tell us about your art," Rachel began, her voice gentle but firm. Laura looked up, her eyes swollen from crying. "What do you mean?"

"Your use of the crimson ribbon," Rachel clarified. "Is there any special significance to it?" Laura's gaze drifted to the floor. "It's just a motif," she said, her voice small. "Something I've used in my work for a while." Rachel's eyes narrowed. "But why that ribbon?" Laura took a deep, shaky breath. "It's… It's just a symbol of pain and loss. It's something that's always resonated with me."

Sam leaned in, his tone more accusatory. "Or did the Scarlet Strangler give it to you?" Laura's eyes snapped up, her expression mixed with fear and anger. "No!" she exclaimed. "I swear, I didn't know about them until they contacted me!" Rachel watched her closely, searching for any crack in her story. Laura's eyes remained steadfast, her voice never wavering.

They decided to give Laura a break, letting her go home with a guard on watch with her. Rachel and Sam retreated to the observation room, the walls closing. "What now?" Rachel asked, her voice tight with frustration. Sam rubbed his jaw, his eyes never leaving Laura through the one-way glass. "We keep pushing," he said. "We can't let them manipulate us."

Chapter 12

A BREAK IN THE CASE

They called in Laura's closest friends and family, hoping to steal some information. Hours they were ticked by the room's tension thickening with each fruitless interview. Rachel's mind was a whirlwind of questions. Why Laura? What was the connection between her art and the killer's MO? The crimson ribbon remained a taunting enigma.

The breakthrough came from an unexpected source: Laura's sister, Emma. She spoke softly, her eyes downcast, her hands trembling. "Laura had a… a stalker," she admitted. "He was obsessed with her art, with the ribbon motif. He sent her messages, talked about it all the time." Rachel's eyes snapped to Sam's. "Did Laura report this?"

Emma looked away. "No, she was scared. She didn't want to make a big deal out of it. She thought he was just a fan and would go away eventually." Rachel's heart sank. Laura had been living in fear, her creativity twisted by a madman's obsession. "What did he say in these messages?" Sam pressed, his voice gruff.

"He talked about how the ribbon represented life and death," Emma whispered, her eyes filling with tears. "How it was the perfect symbol for his… art." Rachel felt bile rise in her throat. The Scarlet Strangler had been watching Laura, studying her, using her art to taunt and manipulate her. "Do you know who this person is?" Rachel asked, her voice gentle.

Emma nodded, her eyes still downcast. "It's Mark," she said, her voice shaking. "Mark Caste llanos. He used to come to Laura's exhibits all the time. He was always so intense, so focused on her work." Rachel and Sam exchanged a look. Mark Caste llanos—it was a name they hadn't heard before. "Is there anything else you can tell us about him?" Rachel prompted.

Emma took a deep breath, gathering her thoughts. "He was… strange," she began. "He'd ask Laura questions about her art, about the ribbon, like he was trying to figure out some hidden meaning. Laura said he was just weird, but she never felt threatened." Rachel's mind raced. A stalker obsessed with Laura's art, specifically the crimson ribbon, could be the link they needed to identify the Scarlet Strangler.

They immediately called for a background check on Mark Caste Llanos. The information that came back was alarming. Mark had a history of assault and restraining orders but nothing that directly connected him to the murders. Rachel's instincts screamed at her to bring him in for questioning. "Sam," she said, her voice firm. "We need to find Mark."

They headed out to Mark's last known address, a shabby apartment complex on the outskirts of town. The tension in the car was palpable as they approached the building. Rachel's gut told her they were getting closer to the truth, but she couldn't shake the feeling that they were also walking into a trap. Laura's words echoed: "They said they'd come for me." Was Mark the Scarlet Strangler, or was he just another pawn in the killer's game?

The apartment was eerily quiet when they knocked. After a tense moment, the door creaked open, revealing a man in his mid-thirties with messy hair and a wild look in his eyes. "Mark Caste llanos?" Rachel asked, her hand resting on her gun. He nodded, his eyes darting between Rachel and Sam. "What's this about?"

They stepped inside, the apartment contrasting with Laura's bright, organized studio. The walls were bare, except for a few pieces of Laura's art, each with a crimson ribbon painted. Rachel's heart hammered in her chest. "We're here to talk about Laura and your interest in her work," Sam said, his voice firm. Mark's eyes lit up with a strange enthusiasm. "Oh, Laura," he murmured, a small smile on his lips.

He led them through a narrow hallway into a dimly lit room that smelled faintly of turpentine and something metallic and unsettling. Rachel's eyes adjusted to the darkness, and she gasped. The walls were lined with paintings depicting the same scene: a woman with a crimson ribbon around her neck, her eyes wide with terror. Each painting was signed with a tattooed hand—identical to the one Laura had described.

"You're a fan of Laura's art," Rachel said, her voice steady despite the horror creeping into her gut. Mark nodded, his eyes gleaming with an intensity that sent a shiver down Rachel's spine. "More than a fan," he corrected, his voice a low rumble. "I'm her muse." Rachel exchanged a glance with Sam, the implications of Mark's words sinking in. Was he confessing? Or was this another twisted layer in the killer's game?

His story weaved a tangled web of obsession and delusion as they talked to Mark. He spoke of speaking to Laura through her art, of guiding her hand to create the perfect symbol of his "work." Rachel felt the tension in the room tighten as they realized Laura had been more than just a victim—she had been an unwitting accomplice in the Scarlet Strangler's twisted artistry.

As Mark spoke, Rachel noticed something peculiar about his hand. A faint line of red ink peeked out from under his sleeve, tracing the edge of his thumb. Her eyes widened. "Let me see your hand," she demanded, her voice steely. Mark's smile faltered, his eyes flicking to the tattoo before he slowly extended his arm.

There it was—the crimson ribbon tattoo, matching the description Laura had given them. Rachel's pulse quickened as the pieces fell into place. Laura had been telling the truth, but it was more twisted than they had imagined. "Sam, get the cuffs," she barked, her eyes never leaving Mark's face. He complied, his movements swift and precise.

Mark's eyes darted to the tattoo, then back to Rachel. The smile was gone, replaced by a look of cold calculation. "You think you're so clever," he sneered. "But you're just pawns in the grand design." Rachel's grip on her gun tightened as Mark began to laugh, a sound that sent chills down her spine.

Sam stepped forward to put the handcuffs around Mark's wrists. "You're coming with us," he said, his voice mixed with disgust and determination. But Mark was one step ahead. He yanked his arm free with a sudden burst of speed, knocking the lamp off the side table. The room plunged into darkness. Rachel heard a scuffle and a thud; then a door slammed shut. "Sam!" Rachel called her hand instinctively, reaching for her gun. "He's getting away!"

They sprinted down the hallway, the echo of Mark's retreating footsteps guiding them. Rachel's heart raced, the weight of the situation pressing down on her. They had been so close to ending this nightmare. The sound of a window shattering pierced the quiet, followed by the distant clang of a fire escape. They burst into the alley to find Mark descending, his silhouette blending into the shadows.

"Freeze!" Rachel shouted, her gun drawn. But he was too quick, leaping from the last rung and sprinting into the night. Rachel took off after him, her shoes slapping against the wet pavement. The alley was a maze of dumpsters and shadowy figures, all potential hiding spots for a man desperate to evade capture. Sam was right behind her, his weapon at the ready. They rounded a corner, and Rachel's eyes narrowed as she spotted a flash of movement.

Mark's figure darted through the narrow spaces between buildings, his footsteps barely audible over the distant hum of the city. Rachel's breath came in ragged gasps, her legs burning as she pushed herself to keep up. They turned down an even darker alley, the only light coming from the occasional flicker of a street lamp. The rain had picked up, plastering her hair to her face and making it hard to see. Rachel's eyes scanned the area, searching for any clue leading them to Mark.

The alley opened up into a small, deserted parking lot. Rachel squinted into the rain, spotting a shadow moving swiftly towards a car parked in the far corner. "There!" she shouted, pointing. Sam nodded, and they both broke into a run. The car's engine roared to life just as they reached it, and Rachel felt the heat of the exhaust as it sped away, leaving them in a cloud of mist and gravel.

They exchanged a frustrated look, their breath misting in the chilly air. Rachel keyed her radio. "Suspect is in a black sedan headed north on Elm Street. Requesting backup immediately." The static-filled response assured them that units were on the way. They took a moment to catch their breath, the adrenaline of the chase still pulsing through their veins.

The rain grew heavier, soaking through their clothes and slick the pavement. Rachel's eyes scanned the lot, looking for any sign Mark had left behind. A crumpled scrap of paper glinted in the puddle beside the dumpster. She bent down, plucking it from the water with a trembling hand. It was a torn page from a sketchbook, the crimson ribbon image stark against the damp paper. Rachel's stomach churned as she recognized Laura's handwriting in the corner. It was a note to Mark, a plea for understanding. Rachel's mind raced, trying to capture the full extent of Laura's involvement.

"This isn't over," Rachel murmured, crumpling the paper. Sam's hand rested on her shoulder, a silent promise of support. They turned back to the apartment, the weight of their failure pressing down on them like the relentless rain. Inside, the room looked even more sinister in the flickering glow of the emergency lights. Rachel approached one of the paintings, studying the crimson ribbon more closely. It wasn't just a detail but a signature, a declaration of ownership over Laura's soul.

Chapter 13

O N THE RUN

As they waited for backup, Rachel couldn't help but feel a pang of pity for Laura. She had been a pawn in Mark's twisted game, her talent exploited for his sick ends. Rachel vowed to find Mark and bring him to justice, not just for the victims but for Laura. Sirens grew louder outside, and the cavalry arrived to sweep the area. Rachel hoped it wasn't too late to save anyone else from becoming part of Mark's macabre art gallery.

The first officers on the scene looked around the apartment in horror, taking in the gruesome display of paintings. Rachel and Sam quickly filled them in on the situation, passing along the description of Mark and the car he'd escaped in. The team split up, some heading to the parking lot to search for the sedan while others began securing the apartment as a crime scene. Rachel felt the walls closing in on her, the weight of their failure to capture Mark palpable in the air.

They stepped outside to wait for the forensics team, but the rain was now a downpour. Rachel's mind was racing, trying to piece together the puzzle of Laura's involvement with Mark. The note in her hand was a tangible connection, a cry for help that had gone unanswered for too long. She smoothed out the wet paper, her eyes scanning the frantic scrawl. Despite her fear, Laura knew the truth about Mark and was drawn into his world. Rachel's heart ached for the woman whose art had been perverted into a tool of terror.

The wail of sirens grew closer, the pulse of blue and red lights painting the alley in a chaotic dance. Rachel stepped into the rain, her eyes on the horizon where Mark had disappeared. She knew they'd find him—his arrogance would be his downfall. He had made himself too visible, too connected to Laura. The crimson ribbon tattoo was more than a mere calling card; it was a declaration of his twisted love.

The rain soaked Rachel's clothes, melding the fabric to her skin and leaving her cold and exposed. Sam hovered nearby, his frustration evident in the tight set of his jaw. Rachel turned to him, the sketch in her hand fluttering in the wind. "We need to find out more about Laura's connection to him," she said, her voice low and determined. "Her art was the key to understanding his mind."

They retreated to their car, the sirens fading into the background as they stepped into the cocoon of relative quiet. Rachel tossed the sketch onto the dashboard, the crimson ribbon stark against the beige upholstery. Sam slammed the door shut, his eyes reflecting the fiery determination in Rachel's. "We'll get him," he assured her. "But we need to tread carefully. He's more dangerous than we thought."

The rain had turned into a downpour, the windshield wipers struggling to keep up with the deluge. Rachel leaned back in her seat, her eyes on the road, searching for any sign of Mark's car. Her mind raced, trying to anticipate his next move. Would he go into hiding? Or would he be bold and try to reach out to Laura again? The thought made her stomach turn. They needed to find him before he could do any more harm.

Sam's phone buzzed with a text message. He glanced at the screen, then back at Rachel. "They've spotted the sedan," he said, his voice tight with excitement. "They're in pursuit." Rachel nodded, gripping the steering wheel. "Good," she murmured. "We can't let him get away."

The chase led them through the labyrinth of the city's streets, the car's headlights cutting through the curtain of rain. Rachel's eyes never left the road, her focus unwavering. She could feel Mark's presence in the air, an evil force taunting them. Every turn they took brought them closer to the truth, but the fear of what they might find grew stronger.

The sedan's taillights grew brighter in the distance as Rachel pushed the car to its limits, her knuckles white on the steering wheel. The rain was a blur, the world outside a canvas of shadows and neon reflections. Sam kept a firm grip on the dashboard, his eyes darting between the GPS and the rearview mirror. "He's headed towards the docks," he said, his voice tense. Rachel's mind raced with scenarios, each more grim than the last. The docks were a notorious hiding spot for the city's worst—where no one would question a missing person.

The car swerved around a corner, tires screeching on the wet asphalt. Rachel's eyes narrowed as she glimpsed the sedan's brake lights flicker on and off. "He's trying to lose us," she murmured. Sam nodded, his hand reaching for the radio. "We've got him boxed in," he said, his voice clear and calm despite the chaos around them. "Backup's five minutes out." Rachel's grip tightened. They couldn't let Mark slip away again, not after what they'd seen, not after Laura.

The sedan's taillights grew more extensive in the rearview mirror, and Rachel floored the gas pedal. The engine roared in response, the car leaping forward like a predator on the hunt. The streets grew narrower, the buildings leaning in as if whispering secrets to each other. Rachel's eyes darted between the road and the GPS, her instincts honed from years of chasing monsters. Mark was clever, but he'd made a mistake— he'd led them to his lair.

As they approached the docks, the rain grew heavier, and the windshield wipers fought a losing battle against the deluge. The air grew thick with the scent of brine and diesel, and the cobblestone streets gave way to cracked asphalt. Rachel's heart pounded in her chest, and her eyes locked on the car ahead. The chase was climaxing, and the stakes were as high as the waves crashing against the shore.

The sedan took a sharp turn, skidding onto a deserted dockside road. Rachel followed, her car's headlights piercing the gloom. The dock was a ghostly specter, the water churning and frothing in the storm's embrace. Rachel spotted Mark's silhouette leaping from the car, disappearing into the shadows between the towering shipping containers. Without a word, she and Sam were out of the car, guns drawn, sprinting after him.

Their feet pounded against the slick ground, the rain stinging their faces as they wove through the labyrinth of metal boxes. Rachel's heart was a drum in her chest, the echo of their pursuit lost in the howling wind. They could see the crimson glow of Mark's taillights up ahead, the car's engine idling like a beast waiting for prey. Rachel's eyes narrowed, her breath coming in harsh gasps. They were so close.

They rounded a corner, and Rachel saw him—his silhouette stark against the backdrop of the stormy harbor. Mark was climbing over a chain-link fence, his movements fluid and practiced. Rachel and Sam leaped out of the car, their shoes splashing in the puddles. Rachel shouted into the wind, "Mark! Stop! We want to talk!" But he didn't turn around. He vaulted over the fence and disappeared into the foggy night.

Their pursuit led them through a maze of shipping containers, the rain now a torrent that soaked their clothes and obscured their vision. Rachel's legs burned with exertion, but she didn't slow down. Mark's car sat there, abandoned, the engine ticking like a clock counting down to an explosion. Rachel's instincts screamed at her to be careful, but she couldn't shake the feeling that they were racing against time.

They approached the fence cautiously, Rachel's gun held firmly in both hands. She signaled to Sam, and together, they vaulted over the barrier, landing in a squat on the other side. The dock was a ghost town; the only sounds were the mournful wail of the wind and the distant crash of waves. Rachel's eyes searched the darkness, trying to spot any hint of movement. The rain had washed away any footprints, leaving them no trail to follow.

"Spread out," Rachel yelled over the storm. "He can't have gone far." They fanned out, their flashlights casting eerie patterns on the wet asphalt. Rachel's heart hammered in her chest, and the crimson ribbon tattoo burned into her mind's eye. Laura's paintings had led them to this desolate place where Mark had tried to elude them. The dock was a maze of containers and shadowy alleys, each a potential hiding spot for a man desperate to evade capture.

The rain lashed at them, making it difficult to see, but Rachel's determination was unshakable. She felt a strange kinship with Laura, a bond formed through shared horror. They had to bring Mark to justice, not just for the sake of the victims but for Laura, too. Rachel's eyes scanned the area, looking for clues leading them to him. She spotted a glint of metal in the distance—a set of keys half-buried in a puddle. Mark's escape had been hasty, leaving a breadcrumb of evidence in his wake.

Sam's radio crackled to life, the voice of their dispatcher cutting through the static. "All units, be advised that the suspect has boarded a cargo ship, the SS Atlantis, docked at berth 17. It's scheduled to leave in 15 minutes." Rachel's eyes widened. "We've got to move," she shouted over the wind. They sprinted towards the ship, their feet pounding the slick dock. Rachel's mind raced—what was Mark planning?

The SS Atlantis loomed before them, a towering metal giant with a gaping maw that promised a quick escape. Rachel and Sam climbed the gangway, their eyes scanning the chaotic scene of dockworkers and machinery. Rachel's instincts screamed at her to find Mark before he disappeared into the ship's bowels. The rain had turned the deck slick, making their pursuit treacherous.

They split up, Rachel heading towards the stern while Sam moved towards the bow. Rachel's flashlight bobbed as she sprinted, casting a beam of light through the sheets of rain. The ship's horn blared, a mournful cry echoing her desperation. The clock was ticking, each second bringing Mark closer to slipping through their grasp.

The deck was a slick dance floor of rain and oil, making every step a battle against gravity. Rachel's eyes scanned the containers, searching for any sign of movement. The wind howled around her, stealing her breath and whipping her hair into a fierce halo. She could feel the ship's engines rumbling beneath her feet, promising Mark's imminent escape.

Her radio crackled, and Sam's voice strained with urgency. "Rachel, I think I've found something!" Rachel sprinted towards the sound, her shoes slipping on the wet metal. Sam was hunched over, his flashlight illuminating a crimson ribbon tied around a thick mooring rope. Rachel's heart skipped a beat. It was a taunt, a twisted message from Mark that he was still watching them, still playing his game.

They had to move fast. Rachel and Sam raced up the stairs to the ship's bridge, the wind screaming through the open hatches. The captain, a grizzled man with a weathered face, barked orders into a radio, his eyes wide with fear. "You've got to stop this ship!" Rachel shouted over the din. "There's a killer on board!"

The captain's gaze flicked to the crimson ribbon in Rachel's hand, and his face paled. He nodded curtly, barking orders to his crew. The engines groaned in protest, the ship's momentum slowing. Rachel's heart sank as she heard the clang of the final ropes being cast off. They were too late.

They sprinted through the ship's corridors, the metal walls echoing with their footsteps. Rachel's mind raced with scenarios, each more dire than the last. Mark had always been one step ahead—how could they catch him now? Sam's radio crackled again, a frantic voice reporting that they had found a cabin with a broken lock. Rachel's pulse quickened. This was it—his final stand.

They burst into the cabin, guns drawn, only to find it empty. Rainwater dripped from their clothes, pooling on the floor. Rachel's eyes scanned the room, searching for any clue to Mark's whereabouts. Then, she saw a crimson ribbon fluttering out of the open porthole. He had gone overboard.

They rushed to the ship's edge, peering into the churning waters below. The rain made it almost impossible to see anything, but Rachel caught a glimpse of a figure in the distance, swimming towards the shadowy form of a nearby dock. "There!" she shouted, pointing. Sam nodded, already moving towards the stairs.

They took them two at a time, their footsteps echoing through the ship's steel belly. The engines' roar grew louder as they descended, the urgency of their mission driving them forward. They had to get to the water level before Mark could escape. Rachel's lungs burned, her legs feeling like lead as they reached the bottom deck. The exit was in sight, the rain beckoning them into the chaos outside.

They burst through the door, the wind and rain slapping them in the face like a cold, wet towel. Rachel squinted into the storm, her eyes searching the water's surface. There! A flash of movement, a ripple in the inky water. Mark's head bobbed up, his strokes powerful and determined. Rachel's finger tightened on the trigger of her gun, her heart racing as she aimed.

But before she could fire, Sam's hand clamped down on her wrist. "We need him alive," he shouted over the storm. Rachel's teeth gritted, but she knew he was right. They needed answers to understand the full extent of Mark's obsession with Laura. They were required to dismantle his twisted world brick by brick.

They sprinted along the dock, the wind pushing against them like a living thing. Rachel's eyes never left Mark's form in the water, his strokes growing more frantic as he neared the shadowy embrace of the shore. The dock lights flickered, casting an eerie glow across the churning waves. Rachel's boots thudded on the wooden planks, each step declaring their pursuit.

As they reached the end of the dock, Rachel spotted a figure on the shore—a woman, her hair plastered to her face, her clothes sodden. Laura. Rachel's heart skipped a beat. Had Mark brought her here? Was she a hostage or an accomplice? Rachel shouted her name, the wind carrying the desperation in her voice. Laura looked up, her eyes wide with terror, the crimson ribbon stark against her pale neck.

They had no time to ponder her role as Mark's head emerged from the water, his eyes wild and feral. Rachel stepped closer to the edge, her gun trained on him. "Stop," she yelled, her voice barely audible over the storm. Mark grinned, his teeth a flash of white in the darkness. He grabbed Laura's arm, pulling her to her feet. "You're too late," he screamed, the wind stealing his words.

Laura's eyes met Rachel's, a silent plea for help. Rachel's finger hovered over the trigger, the weight of the decision heavy on her heart. But she knew—she couldn't risk Laura's life. Not now, not after all she'd suffered. "Let her go," Rachel demanded, her voice steady despite the rage within her.

Mark's grin widened, a sadistic twist of his lips. "You think you can save her?" he shouted, the wind carrying his taunt. "She's been mine from the start!" Rachel's mind raced, searching for a way to diffuse the situation. Laura's art had been a window into Mark's soul, but now it was a noose around her neck, and Rachel feared she might never break free.

The rain battered them as Mark dragged Laura towards the edge of the dock. Rachel took a cautious step closer, her eyes never leaving Mark's.

"We just want to talk," Rachel yelled, keeping her voice calm. "We can help you both." Mark's laughter was cold and cruel, a stark contrast to the desperate cries of the storm. "Help?" he sneered. "You don't understand. Laura and I are one. Her art is my soul made manifest."

The wind picked up, whipping Rachel's hair into her face. She squinted through the rain, her heart racing. Laura's eyes were filled with fear and confusion, her grip on Mark's arm tightening. Rachel could see the turmoil within her, the struggle to break free from his twisted embrace. "Let her go," Rachel demanded again, her voice stronger this time. "This ends now."

Mark's eyes narrowed, and Rachel saw their madness—a wild, untamed fury plaguing them for too long. He yanked Laura closer to the water's edge, the waves crashing below them. Rachel took a deep breath, her mind racing for a way to save Laura without risking her life. The ship's horn blared again, a mournful sound that seemed to echo Rachel's fear.

Suddenly, Laura's gaze found Rachel's, and in that moment, Rachel saw a flicker of something—determination, perhaps. Laura jerked her arm free from Mark's grip, and with a primal scream, she pushed him backward. Rachel's heart stopped as Mark teetered on the edge of the dock, the storm's fury seeming to hold him in place for a brief, eternal moment. Then, with a splash, he disappeared into the black water below.

Laura collapsed to her knees, the crimson ribbon still wrapped around her neck, a symbol of the horror she'd endured. Rachel rushed to her side, her gun lowering as she assessed the situation. Laura's eyes searched Rachel's, seeking reassurance and understanding. Rachel offered her a hand, and Laura took it, her grip surprisingly firm. They stood together, the rain a cacophony around them, the wind a relentless force pushing against their backs.

The water churned where Mark had fallen, but no sign of him

resurfacing. Rachel's heart was a hammer in her chest, her mind racing with the implications of what had just happened. Had Laura finally broken free from Mark's grip, or was this a ploy, a twisted part of his grand design? Rachel's gaze never left Laura's, looking for any sign of the woman she had come to know through her art.

Chapter 14

THE IMPACT OF TRAUMA

"You're safe now," Rachel said, her voice gentle but firm. Laura nodded, the rain mixing with her tears as she shivered uncontrollably. Rachel wrapped her jacket around Laura's shoulders, the warmth contrasting with the coldness leaving them. "Let's get you somewhere warm," Rachel murmured, leading Laura back towards the car.

As they approached the vehicle, Rachel's eyes remained on the water, where Mark had disappeared, swallowed by the raging waves. Her mind raced with the possibility that he might still be alive and waiting for them to lower their guard. But she couldn't let fear control her now. Laura needed her.

They climbed into the car, Rachel's eyes scanning the rearview mirror for any sign of movement. Laura sat quietly in the back, the crimson ribbon a stark reminder of the horrors she'd faced. Rachel started the engine, and the heater's warmth gently embraced against the cold. She glanced at Sam, his eyes reflecting the gravity of the situation. "We need to get her to a safe place," Rachel said firmly.

Sam nodded, his gaze never leaving Laura in the mirror. "Agreed," he said, his voice tight with tension. "But we can't just let him get away." Rachel knew he was right—Mark was still out there, a dangerous loose end. But Laura's safety was their priority. Rachel's mind raced, trying to devise a plan to protect Laura and bring Mark to justice.

They drove through the storm-lashed streets, the windshield wipers fighting a courageous battle against the rain. Laura's shivering grew less violent, but the haunted look in her eyes remained. Rachel reached back, her hand resting comfortingly on Laura's arm. "You're not alone," she assured her. Laura offered a small, shy smile, the weight of her ordeal etched into every line of her face.

As they pulled into the parking lot, the precinct was a beacon of light and warmth. Rachel could feel the tension coiling tighter in her gut. The interrogation room was just a few steps away, and she knew that Laura's nightmare was far from over. But she also knew that it was the first step towards healing, towards justice.

Laura was taken to a private room to get cleaned up and warmed. Rachel watched her go, feeling a pang of guilt for the pain she had endured. She turned to Sam, her eyes determined. "We need to find him," she said, her voice low and urgent. "We can't let him vanish again."

Sam nodded gravely. "Agreed. We'll canvas the docks and get divers in the water. He can't have gotten far." Rachel knew they had to act fast before Mark could regroup and disappear into the city's shadows.

Inside the precinct, the warmth and bustle of activity felt alien after the stormy chase. Rachel's thoughts remained with Laura, her mind racing with questions about the depth of Laura's involvement and what Mark had subjected her to.

As they approached the briefing room, Rachel saw a blur of uniforms and heard the cacophony of radios and phones. She knew the search was already in full swing. The sergeant looked up from his desk, his expression a mix of relief and urgency. "We've got reports of a man matching Mark's description in the area," he bellowed. "He can't have gotten far."

Rachel and Sam exchanged a grim look. They had to find Mark before he could harm anyone else before he could twist more lives with his sick games. Rachel's mind was a whirlwind of thoughts—how many other women had suffered under his watch? How many had never had the chance to break free like Laura?

Chapter 15

A RACE AGAINST TIME

The sergeant handed them fresh raincoats and updated them on the search perimeter. "We've got K-9 units and a helicopter en route," he said, his voice grim. "We'll leave no stone unturned." Rachel nodded, her resolve hardening. Laura's art had been a map to Mark's twisted soul, and now it was their weapon to bring him down.

They stepped back into the storm, the rain a relentless barrage that seemed to mirror the chaos in Rachel's mind. The dock was a blur of blue and yellow lights, officers shouting orders over the storm's din. Rachel's eyes searched the water, the crimson ribbon now a fiery brand seared into her memory.

The K-9 unit arrived, the dogs' eager barks piercing the air as they were released from their vehicles. Rachel watched as they tore off into the night, their handlers in hot pursuit. The helicopter's spotlight sliced through the darkness, casting elongated shadows that danced on the water's surface. The hunt was on.

Rachel and Sam took cover under a nearby awning, their eyes scanning the chaotic scene. Rachel's mind was a whirlwind of hypotheses.

Had Mark survived the fall? Was he hiding somewhere nearby, watching them? Or had the water claimed him, taking him out to sea to be lost forever?

The rain was a relentless drumbeat, a rhythm that matched Rachel's chest pounding. She knew that every second counted; every moment that passed increased the likelihood of Mark slipping through their fingers. Rachel's eyes narrowed as she thought of Laura, still in the precinct, her life forever changed by Mark's obsession.

Suddenly, the radio on Sam's belt crackled to life, the static parting to reveal a voice, urgent and strained. Rachel's heart skipped a beat as she listened. "We've found something, but it's not Mark. It's another body." Rachel's stomach dropped, the words echoing in her ears like a death knell.

They sprinted through the rain, following the radio's frantic directions, their steps echoing off the slick cobblestone streets. The dock's lights grew brighter, casting an eerie glow over the scene ahead. In the murky water, a group of officers had gathered, their flashlights illuminating a grim discovery. Rachel's eyes widened in horror as she saw the crimson ribbon tangled in the lifeless form's hair.

The body was a young woman, her face a mask of terror, forever frozen in the throes of a violent death. Rachel felt the air leave her lungs as she recognized her—one of Laura's missing models, her art brought to life in the most dreadful way possible. Mark had left her as a message, a twisted trophy of his elusiveness. Rachel's grip on her gun tightened, anger and grief warring within her.

The storm raged on, indifferent to the tragedy unfolding on the docks. Rachel's eyes swept the scene, searching for any clue that Mark had been there. The crimson ribbon, a chilling reminder of Laura's art, was wrapped around the victim's neck, a twisted emblem of his obsession. Rachel's mind raced, piecing together the puzzle. This wasn't just about evading capture—Mark was taunting them, leaving a trail of destruction in his wake.

The radio crackled again, the voice on the other end strained. "We've found another one." Rachel's stomach lurched. How many more would there be? Each discovery brought a new wave of dread. She knew Mark's game was far from over, his sick fascination with Laura's art a dark tapestry of fear and control. The body count grew, each one a testament to his depravity.

They sprinted through the storm, the wind and rain a torrent that seemed to mirror the chaos of their mission. The dock's lights grew closer, a grim beacon guiding them to the next horrific scene. As they approached, Rachel could see the huddled forms of officers, their flashlights casting a morbid ballet of shadows. Her heart raced, anticipating the worst.

The second body lay in the water, a crimson ribbon wound around its neck, a ghastly reflection of Laura's art. Rachel felt a knot of horror tightens in her stomach. "It's her," she murmured, recognizing the young woman's features from Laura's paintings. Sam's jaw clenched, his eyes hard with determination. "This isn't over," he said, his voice a promise of retribution.

The radio squawked again, the dispatcher's voice urgent. "We've got a report of a suspicious person matching Mark's description near the marina." Rachel's pulse quickened. The marina was a labyrinth of boats and piers, a perfect hiding place. "We're on it," she responded, her voice firm. They took off at a run, their boots splashing through puddles, the rain a relentless drumbeat on their backs.

As they approached the marina, Rachel's eyes darted between the shadowy figures huddled under awnings and the boats that rocked gently in their moorings. The rain had eased to a steady drizzle, but the wind still howled, carrying the scent of salt and diesel. Rachel's flashlight danced over the slick wooden docks, searching for any sign of Mark.

The radio on Sam's belt crackled again, the dispatcher's voice taut with tension. "We've got a visual on the suspect. He's heading towards the north end of the marina." Rachel's pulse spiked. They were close. She could feel it. The chase had become personal—not just about capturing a killer, but about stopping the monster that had tormented Laura and so many others.

Chapter 16

THE DESPERATE PURSUIT

They sprinted through the maze of piers, their flashlights slicing through the misty darkness. Rachel's eyes scanned the water, searching for any movement, any sign of Mark's escape. Each splash of water on the docks seemed to echo his taunts. The rain had turned the world into a shadowy battleground, each puddle a potential trap.

The radio crackled again, the voice now a harsh whisper. "We've got another one." Rachel's stomach plummeted. Mark's madness claimed another innocent life. She almost felt his presence, an evil force toying with them, leaving a gruesome breadcrumb trail. They had to find him before he could claim anyone else.

They pushed through the storm, the wind whipping Rachel's hair across her face. Each step brought them closer to the marina, the air thick with the scent of rain and the metallic tang of fear. Rachel's eyes darted between the boats, searching for any sign of movement. The fog had thickened, turning the marina into a ghostly tableau of shadows and echoes.

The radio squawked, the dispatcher's voice grim. "We've found another one." Rachel's stomach twisted. Not Mark, but another victim, another life snuffed out by his twisted games. Sam's pace didn't falter, his eyes scanning the horizon as they approached the north end of the marina. Rachel's mind raced, deciphering the pattern to anticipate Mark's next move.

The fog had thickened, making seeing more than a few feet ahead tricky. Rachel's flashlight cut through the gloom, illuminating the slick wooden planks beneath their feet. The boats bobbed eerily in the water, the clang of their chains against the metal poles a mournful symphony. Each shadow seemed to hold a new terror, and each sound was a potential clue.

The north end of the marina loomed ahead, a place where the water met the city's edge in a tangled embrace of steel and rope. Rachel felt the weight of each victim's life in her chest, a heavy burden that fueled her determination. Mark had turned the docks into a macabre art gallery, displaying his twisted creations for the world. But Rachel knew the truth—these were not mere art pieces; they were lives snuffed out by a madman's obsession.

The fog clung to the water like a shroud, obscuring the line between the living and the dead. Rachel's flashlight danced over the dock's canvas, revealing a tableau of rain-soaked planks and shadowy vessels. Each pier they passed was a silent testament to the horrors here, each slack mooring line whispering a story of loss. Mark's canvas was vast, and Rachel feared the extent of his masterpiece.

They reached the north end, where the city's edge kissed the marina in a morbid embrace. The fog thickened, a smothering blanket that muffled the world's cries. Rachel's heart pounded in her chest, each pulse echoing the hammering of the rain on the water's surface. The dock's end was a chilling sight, the final brushstroke in Mark's macabre painting. Rachel spotted a crimson ribbon fluttering in the breeze like a forsaken banner there.

Her flashlight beam followed the ribbon's trail, revealing a series of piers that stretched out into the abyss like the skeletal fingers of a drowning giant. Each one is a potential stage for Mark's sick exhibition. Rachel's boots thudded on the wooden planks, echoing through the silent night. The docks had become a gruesome gallery of his iniquity; each slips a somber aisle displaying his twisted creations.

They moved methodically; their eyes peeled for any movement, any sign of their elusive quarry. Rachel could feel the weight of each lifeless form they'd found, the crimson ribbons a gruesome signature on Mark's canvas of death. The rain had abated to a gentle patter, the only sound now the lapping of the water against the pilings and the occasional groan of the boats as they swayed in the swells.

The fog had lifted slightly, revealing a solitary figure at the end of the furthest pier. Rachel's heart skipped a beat as she recognized Mark, his silhouette framed by the moon's weak light. He stood with his back to them, seemingly lost in contemplation of the water's inky depths. Rachel and Sam cautiously approached, their every step measured, their breaths shallow.

As they neared, Rachel could see the crimson ribbon fluttering from his hand, a twisted extension of the ones that had bound his victims. The dock creaked under their combined weight, a mournful tune that seemed to echo the sorrow of the lives he'd claimed. Rachel's eyes were drawn to the water below, where the ribbons of the slain danced in the murky currents, forever entwined in Mark's macabre artistry.

The pier stretched into the abyss, the darkness of the water a stark contrast to the stark reality of the moment. Rachel felt the weight of each lifeless form they'd found, each a silent testament to Mark's twisted muse. The wind whispered through the rigging of the boats, a mournful symphony that seemed to lament the lives lost to his madness. Each slap of water against the pilings was a reminder of the souls claimed by his deadly brush.

They approached the figure slowly, their flashlights converging on Mark's silhouette. Rachel could see the crimson ribbon in his hand, fluttering like a bloody flag in the breeze. "Mark," she called out, her voice steady despite the tremble in her hand. "We need to talk."

He turned, his eyes wild, and Rachel saw the desperation in his face. He was cornered, his masterpiece of terror unraveling before him. "You don't understand," he shouted over the wind. "It's not about the art—the connection, the power!"

Rachel took a step closer, her voice steady. "Mark, you need to come with us. Laura's safe now."

Mark's eyes darted between Rachel and Sam, his grip on the crimson ribbon tightening. "I need to talk to Laura," he insisted, his voice strained. "It's the only way to explain."

Rachel's mind raced. Laura was in no condition to face Mark, not now, not ever. But she knew she had to keep him talking, to keep him from doing anything rash. "What is it you need to say to her?" Rachel asked, her voice measured.

Mark stepped closer, the ribbon fluttering like a crimson flame in the moonlight. "I'm her muse," he whispered, his eyes intense. "Her art is a reflection of me, of us. Without me, she's nothing." Rachel felt a chill run down her spine. The depth of his delusion was more profound than she had imagined.

"What do you mean, 'without you, she's nothing'?" Rachel's voice was calm, but her mind was racing. Laura had been strong enough to break free, to push him into the stormy water. Mark's obsession had twisted their relationship into something dark and unrecognizable.

Mark took a step closer, his eyes feverishly searching Rachel's face. "Her art, it's me. She paints her fear, her desperation, because of me. I'm the muse that brings her to life. Without me, she's just a forgotten artist." Rachel's grip on her gun tightened, her knuckles white. Laura was so much more than Mark's muse; she was a survivor and a warrior.

"You're wrong," Rachel said firmly. "Laura is a brilliant artist in her own right. She doesn't need you for her art or her existence." Mark's expression twisted into a snarl, his hand clenching the crimson ribbon. Rachel could see the fury bubbling beneath the surface, the fragility of his ego laid bare.

"You don't understand," he spat. "Our bond is unbreakable. She needs me just as much as I need her." Rachel took a step closer, her voice low and dangerous. "What you had with Laura was not a bond. It was obsession and manipulation."

Sam moved in from the side, his flashlight bouncing off the slick planks. "Mark, it's over," he said, his voice firm. "We have evidence, we have witnesses. There's nowhere for you to run." Rachel watched Mark's face contort, the rage and desperation playing out like a macabre puppet show.

"You don't get it," Mark yelled, the ribbon flapping wildly in his hand. "Without her, I'm nothing!" Rachel took a step closer, her eyes never leaving Mark's. "Without you, Laura is free," she countered, her voice steady. "Free from your games, your obsession."

Mark's laugh was manic, the wind whipping it away into the stormy night. "You think you know her," he spat. "But she's been playing you all along. She's the brains, the artist. I'm just her muse." Rachel felt a flicker of doubt, but she pushed it aside. Laura had survived Mark's torment; she wouldn't be the mastermind behind it.

"You're wrong," Rachel said firmly, her voice cutting through the storm's din. "Laura is a victim, not a partner in your twisted games." But Mark's words had planted a seed of doubt, and Rachel couldn't shake the feeling that there was more to this tangled web than met the eye. Laura's art had been a cry for help, a silent scream that Rachel had been too slow to hear.

Mark stepped backward, the ribbon fluttering like a crimson flame in the wind. "You've been played, detective," he cackled, his eyes gleaming with malice. "She's the mastermind, the puppeteer pulling your strings. I'm just the canvas she uses to paint her madness." Rachel's heart raced as she processed the revelation, her mind racing through the clues they'd uncovered, the art that had led them here.

Could it be true? Had Laura been orchestrating this twisted dance all along, using Mark as a pawn in her own sick game? Rachel's eyes searched the water below, the ribbons of the slain a haunting reminder of the lives lost to their obsession. Laura had painted fear and desperation, but was it her own or a reflection of the horrors she'd wrought?

Rachel's thoughts raced, trying to reconcile the gentle, traumatized woman she'd met with the cold-hearted mastermind Mark claimed her to be. But the doubt grew, weaving its tendrils through her mind like the crimson ribbon bounding each victim. Laura's art was dark, but was it born of her own darkness or merely a mirror to Mark's?

Rachel took a deep breath, pushing the doubt aside. "Mark, we know you're responsible for these crimes," she said firmly. "The evidence is clear." She stepped closer, her flashlight beam illuminating the desperation in his eyes. "You're the one we're after."

He took another step back, the crimson ribbon fluttering like a taunt in the wind. "You're wrong," he shouted. "Laura, she's the one in control. She's the artist, the mastermind. I'm just her muse!" Rachel felt the floor drop out from under her. Was it possible that Laura had orchestrated this twisted masquerade? The gentle, traumatized woman she'd consoled, the haunting art that had led them here—was it all a facade?

Her mind reeled, sifting through the evidence, the conversations, the emotions. Laura's art was indeed dark, but Rachel had seen genuine fear in her eyes when Mark was mentioned. Was that fear for herself, or was it a calculated performance? Rachel's hand tightened around her gun, her heart racing. Laura had painted a picture of desperation, but was it her own, or had she painted Rachel into a corner of doubt?

Chapter 17

A WEB OF LIES

Mark took another step backward, the crimson ribbon wrapping around his hand like a scarlet snake. "You're too late," he sneered. "You'll never understand our bond. She needed me to take the fall, to be the villain in her story. But I'm a strong swimmer," he bragged, a hint of madness glinting in his eyes. "I've been swimming away from your grasp all along."

Rachel's eyes narrowed, her thoughts racing. Laura had painted a picture of fear, but was it indeed for herself, or was it a cunning ploy to cast Mark as the monster while she remained in the shadows? The revelation was a dagger to Rachel's gut, but she couldn't let it show. She had to keep Mark talking and keep him focused on her and Sam.

"You're wrong," Rachel said, her voice laced with doubt she didn't feel. "Laura had nothing to do with this. She's a victim, not a killer." Mark's smirk grew, the wind teasing the ribbon around his fist.

"Look at her art," he goaded. "Look at the fear, the desperation. She painted her story, and I played my part. But she didn't count on me being more than a muse." Rachel's mind raced, recalling Laura's apartment's vivid, haunting images. The crimson ribbon in Mark's hand fluttered like a macabre confetti, a silent testament to his claim.

"You're wrong," Rachel said again, her voice firm. "We have witnesses, evidence. You can't escape justice." Mark's laugh was a harsh bark that pierced the stormy silence. "Justice?" he spat. "You don't know the first thing about it. You're just a pawn in her game, a player in her art." Rachel felt the weight of his words, the doubt he had sown now a heavy burden.

The wind picked up, sending the ribbon spiraling like a crimson tornado. Rachel's eyes followed it, her mind racing. Laura had painted fear, but was it her own or a masterstroke of manipulation? Rachel had to believe in Laura's innocence and hold onto the hope that she hadn't been fooled.

But Mark's words echoed in her mind, a persistent drumbeat of doubt. "The night in the park," Rachel began, her voice barely audible over the storm. "When Laura was found, she had set up a meeting with you. Did she know we would be there?"

Mark's smile grew, a chilling sight in the dim moonlight. "Oh, she knew," he said, his voice filled with a twisted sense of triumph. "It was all part of her grand design. She's been orchestrating this dance, leading you on a merry chase. She's the artist, you see, and we're all just her pawns."

Rachel's heart pounded in her chest as she struggled to maintain her composure. Laura had set up Mark, but had she also set Rachel up? Was Rachel another character in Laura's twisted narrative, a detective blinded by her empathy? The thought was like a slap in the face, cold and brutal. But Rachel couldn't let it show. She had to keep Mark talking and find a way to unravel this tangled web of deceit.

"You're wrong," Rachel said, her voice a tightrope walk between certainty and doubt. "Laura was a victim. She was scared that night in the park. She was running from you." Mark's eyes narrowed, the crimson ribbon fluttering in the wind like a scarlet challenge.

"Or perhaps," he mused, "she was running toward you. It is a perfect setup: a tragic heroine in need of rescue. And you, the brave detective, so eager to play the role." Rachel felt a chill. Had Laura orchestrated that night, painted herself into the canvas of her own horror story? It was a twist Rachel hadn't anticipated, a dark reflection of the art she had come to see as a plea for help.

As Rachel held Mark's gaze, Sam moved with the precision of a cat burglar, his steps silent on the slick dock. Rachel's eyes never left Mark's, her voice a steady counterpoint to the storm's howl. "Laura's a victim, not a killer." But even as she spoke, Rachel felt the doubt coil around her like the crimson ribbon in Mark's hand.

Sam edged closer, his movements calculated, his eyes on Mark's every twitch. Rachel knew her partner was assessing the situation and looking for an opening. Each step he took was a deliberate dance, a silent countdown to the moment he would make his move. The air between them was thick with anticipation, a palpable force that seemed to pulse with the rhythm of Rachel's racing heart.

Mark's eyes darted from Rachel to Sam and back again, his mind racing as he tried to anticipate their next move. Rachel could see the cogs turning, the wheels of his madness trying to create a new escape plan. But Rachel wasn't about to let him slip away. She kept her focus on his eyes, her voice a steady stream of words that kept him engaged, kept him from looking over his shoulder.

Sam took his cue, moving with the grace of a panther stalking its prey. Each step was a silent promise of the end of Mark's twisted reign. Rachel's heart was a drum in her chest, her eyes never leaving Mark's as she watched Sam's reflection in the water below. The crimson ribbon was a blur in Mark's hand, a macabre conductor's baton as he talked.

Rachel knew she had to keep his attention and keep him from seeing the net closing in.

"Your art," Rachel said, her voice a soothing lullaby in the storm's din. "It's beautiful, but the fear, the pain—it's not what makes it powerful." Mark leaned in, his eyes gleaming with malicious delight. Rachel felt the dock creak under their weight, a silent protest to the horrors they were discussing. "The fear," Rachel continued, "it's a mask. Laura's true strength is in her survival, not the darkness you brought into her life."

Sam took that moment, his hand darting like a viper's strike. He grabbed Mark's wrist, the one holding the crimson ribbon, twisting it until Mark's grip loosened. The ribbon fell to the water; a scarlet snake slipped into the abyss. Rachel stepped closer, her gun trained on Mark's chest. "It's over," she said, her voice a storm's calm eye. "You're not a muse; you're a monster."

Mark's eyes widened in surprise, the madness momentarily eclipsed by reality's harsh light. Rachel saw the flicker of fear in his gaze, the first genuine emotion she had seen since they had started this twisted dance. He had been so focused on Rachel, so confident in his delusions, that he had forgotten about Sam.

Sam's handcuffs clicked into place around Mark's wrists, a metallic echo in the silent night. Rachel's eyes never left Mark's face, watching the emotions play like a macabre puppet show. First shock, then anger, and finally a resigned acceptance that his grand performance had ended. The wind howled around them, a mournful dirge for the lives he had claimed, the dreams he had shattered.'

As Rachel read Mark his rights, she couldn't help but think of Laura, the gentle artist whose soul had been marred by his twisted muse. Rachel's heart ached for her, the pain she had endured, and the doubt that now shadowed Rachel's understanding of their relationship. Was Laura indeed the mastermind, the puppeteer pulling Mark's strings? Or was she a pawn in her own game, a victim of her creation?

With Mark secured, Rachel and Sam turned their attention to the water, the crimson ribbon lost to the dark embrace of the sea. Rachel's thoughts were a tumult, a storm of doubt and anger. She had been so sure of Laura's innocence, so focused on saving her, that she had missed the signs of a deeper, more sinister plot.

They escorted Mark back to the precinct, his manic laughter trailing behind them like a sinister echo. Rachel's mind raced with questions she had never dared to ask. Laura's art had been a window into her soul, but what if Rachel had been looking through a distorted lens? Was the fear and desperation indeed Laura's, or was it a mask she had painted for Rachel to see?

Chapter 18

Once at the station, Rachel sat in the interrogation room, watching Laura's eyes as Mark was brought in. Laura's gaze was vacant, her hand trembling slightly as it rested on the table. Rachel searched for any flicker of recognition, any hint of the mastermind Mark had claimed her to be. But all she saw was the same haunted look she had seen the first time they met.

Mark was placed in a chair across from Laura, his cuffs rattling as he was secured. Rachel stepped into the room, her eyes locked onto Laura's. "Do you know him?" Rachel asked gently, her voice contrasting with the storm raging in her thoughts. Laura's eyes widened, a single tear trailing down her cheek.

"He's the one," Laura whispered, her voice barely audible. Rachel felt a flicker of relief, but the doubt remained. Was Laura acting, or was she indeed a survivor? Rachel's gaze shifted to Mark, whose smug smile had been replaced by a furrowed brow. He stared at Laura angrily, confused, as if he couldn't believe she had turned on him.

"Laura," Rachel began, her voice softer than intended. "Is there anything you'd like to tell us?" Laura's eyes met Rachel's, and at that moment, Rachel saw the depth of her pain. Laura's voice was shaky, but the words were clear. "I painted what he made me feel," she said, her hand trembling. "The fear, the desperation—it was all for him." Rachel felt the weight of Laura's words, the truth resonating deeply. Laura was a victim, not a mastermind.

The interrogation room was silent save for the muffled sounds of the storm outside and the distant clanging of the precinct's doors. Rachel's mind reeled with the implications of Laura's confession. The art had been a cry for help, a silent scream at night. Rachel had heard it, but had she truly understood it? Laura had painted her fear and pain, and Rachel had almost missed the real monster before her.

"But the crimson ribbon," Rachel said, her voice tentative. "Why did you use it in your art?" Laura's eyes dropped to her trembling hands, her voice barely a whisper. "It was his signature," she said. "He liked to leave it as a reminder of what he had done and could still do." Rachel's stomach twisted at the thought of Mark's twisted sense of artistry, the lives he had claimed as part of his sick masterpiece.

"I had to include it," Laura continued, her voice gaining strength. "So when someone found my art, they would know the truth. That it wasn't just about me, but about all the others he had hurt." Rachel admired Laura's courage, using her trauma to fight against the monster trying to claim her.

Mark's smug expression had dissolved into one of rage. "You were mine!" he roared, straining against his cuffs. "You painted for me!" Laura didn't flinch, her eyes steady on Rachel's. Rachel knew at that moment that Laura had indeed painted for Mark, but not in the way he believed. Her art was a testament to her survival, a silent declaration of war against the darkness he had brought into her world.

Rachel's thoughts swirled like the fog outside. Laura had been the hunted, the canvas for Mark's sick muse. Rachel had been the detective, driven by a need to protect, to save. And now, as she looked at Laura, she realized she had been the audience all along, drawn into a macabre performance she hadn't fully understood.

"Why did you help him?" Rachel asked, her voice barely above a whisper. Laura's eyes searched Rachel's, looking for something—understanding, perhaps. "I didn't have a choice," Laura said, her voice shaking. "He said if I didn't, he'd hurt more people. I thought if I painted his fears and showed him the horror of his actions, he'd stop." Rachel's heart ached for the young woman's naivety, her desperate hope that art could exorcise the demons within Mark.

"But it only made it worse," Laura continued, trembling. "He liked it. He said it made him feel alive like he was part of something greater." Rachel felt a cold knot form in her stomach. Laura had been a pawn, a tragic heroine caught in Mark's twisted narrative. Rachel's thoughts raced, trying to piece together the puzzle of Laura's art, her silent cries for help.

"I had to keep painting," Laura said, her eyes never leaving Rachel's. "It was the only way to keep him close, understand him, maybe find a way to save myself and others." Rachel reached out, placing a gentle hand on Laura's arm. "You're not to blame for this," she assured her. "You're a survivor." Laura's eyes searched Rachel's, seeking the truth in her words.

The silence in the room was deafening, and the storm outside was a stark reminder of the chaos Mark had brought into their lives. Rachel knew they had to unravel this web of deceit, bring justice for the lives he had taken, and ensure Laura's safety once and for all. "We'll make sure he can't hurt anyone else," Rachel promised, her voice firm. Laura nodded, a hint of a smile ghosting across her lips.

Rachel stepped out of the interrogation room, her mind racing with questions that needed answers. She needed to understand Laura's role in this twisted tale to uncover the truth behind the art that had become a silent confession. Sam followed, his eyes filled with anger and confusion "What do we do now?" he asked, his voice tight with tension. Rachel took a deep breath, the scent of rain and saltwater lingering in the air.

"We keep digging," Rachel said, her voice firm. "We need to find out if Laura was just a pawn or if she had a hand in this." They walked through the bustling precinct, the sounds of phones ringing and officers talking a stark contrast to the quiet resolve in Rachel's voice. "We can't let our emotions cloud our judgment." Sam nodded, his eyes never leaving Rachel's.

They returned to Laura's apartment, where Rachel had first seen the crimson ribbon. The artwork on the walls seemed to watch as they moved through the space, each piece a silent witness to the horrors Laura had endured. Rachel studied the paintings with new eyes, looking for signs of the woman beneath the victim, searching for the artist who had painted her fear.

As Rachel scrutinized the art, her gaze fell upon a piece she had overlooked. It was a self-portrait of Laura, the crimson ribbon wound around her wrist, a look of determination in her eyes. Rachel felt a chill run down her spine. Had Laura sent her a message all along, a clue to the depth of her involvement? Rachel stepped closer, her heart racing as she examined the canvas. The brushstrokes were sharp, almost violent, starkly contrasting the softness of Laura's features.

The more Rachel studied the painting, the more she realized she had looked at Laura's art through a distorted lens. The fear and desperation weren't just Mark's doing—they were Laura's own emotions, painted into existence to manipulate Rachel's perception. Rachel's stomach twisted. How could she have been so blind? Laura had been playing her, using her empathy as a shield. Rachel felt anger and betrayal, but she pushed it aside. Her job was to find the truth, no matter how painful.

The painting was a revelation, a mirror reflecting Rachel's doubts and biases. Laura had painted herself into the role of the victim, but the crimson ribbon wrapped around her wrist told a different story. It was a declaration of power, a silent scream of control in a world where she had none. Rachel's eyes burned with the need to understand, to piece together the puzzle that was Laura's psyche.

With trembling hands, Rachel pulled out her phone and called the precinct. "We need to interview Laura again," she said, her voice cold and hard. "Her art isn't just a cry for help. It's a confession." Sam's eyes widened, the gravity of the situation sinking in. Laura had been playing them, using her art to weave a narrative that painted Mark as the villain and herself as the innocent victim. Rachel felt a knot of anger coil in her stomach, but she pushed it down. They had to be sure and had to have irrefutable evidence before they could act.

Chapter 19

A DEADLY DISCOVERY

As they waited for backup, Rachel couldn't help but study the self-portrait again. Laura's eyes in the painting seemed to follow her, a silent accusation of her failure to see the truth. Rachel had been so focused on Mark, so sure of Laura's innocence, that she had missed the signs of a darker collaboration. The crimson ribbon was a thread that connected them all, a symbol of the tangled web of manipulation and deceit spun in this quiet house.

The minutes stretched into an eternity, Rachel's mind racing with questions and doubt. What had Laura's art indeed been? A plea for salvation or a clever ploy to evade detection? Rachel felt sick at the thought that she had been a pawn in Laura's game, her empathy a tool to be used and discarded. But she had to be sure; she had to find proof to confirm her suspicions.

As the officers arrived, Rachel's eyes remained glued to the self-portrait, the crimson ribbon stark against Laura's pale skin. The painting was a manifesto of control, a silent declaration of Laura's complicity in Mark's crimes. Rachel's heart ached as she realized that the gentle artist she had come to know was not the helpless victim she had believed but a woman who had embraced the darkness that had haunted her.

When Laura was brought in, Rachel could see the smugness in her eyes, the satisfaction of a puppeteer watching her marionettes dance to her tune. Rachel's stomach twisted, but she maintained her calm demeanor, her voice firm as she began the interrogation. "Why?" Rachel asked the question, echoing through the small room. Laura's gaze remained defiant, a chilling reflection of the monster Mark had claimed she was.

"Why?" Laura echoed, her voice a mocking whisper. "Because art is power, Detective. And fear is the purest form of inspiration." Rachel felt the blood drain from her face as Laura's words hit like a sledgehammer. All along, Rachel had been fooled by the person she had vowed to protect, her biases blurring the lines between victim and perpetrator. Laura's art had been a masterful deception, a canvas of lies painted with the crimson ribbon of fear.

The room was stark, the fluorescent lights flickering above their heads, casting a cold glow on Laura's smug expression. Rachel's mind raced back to every conversation, every painting she had studied, searching for signs she had overlooked. Laura had played the part of the broken artist to perfection, using Rachel's empathy as a ladder to climb out of the cage Mark had built around her. The realization was a bitter pill, a knife twisting in Rachel's gut.

The evidence laid out before Rachel was undeniable—sketches of the crime scenes and detailed plans of Mark's movements, all marked with the crimson ribbon symbolizing their twisted partnership. Rachel felt a wave of nausea wash over her as she realized that Laura had been orchestrating the events, using her art as a smoke screen. Each brushstroke, each drop of paint, had been a step closer to the horror that had unfolded before their eyes.

Laura's eyes remained cold and defiant as Rachel sifted through the damning evidence. Rachel's mind reeled with the revelation. The gentle, traumatized artist she had come to care for was a cold, calculating killer, playing on Rachel's emotions to maintain her cover. The crimson ribbon that had once been a symbol of Laura's fear had become a tool of manipulation, a red thread weaving through the fabric of Rachel's reality, twisting it into a monstrous tapestry of deceit.

"You used me," Rachel said, her voice thick with anger and betrayal. Laura's smile grew, a chilling sight that sent a shiver down Rachel's spine. "Used you?" Laura repeated, her tone mocking. "You were just a piece in our masterpiece, Detective. A necessary element to complete the narrative." Rachel felt a knot of horror tighten in her stomach as she realized the depth of Laura's depravity.

The room grew smaller as Rachel studied Laura, trying to reconcile the woman before her with the one she had believed in so fiercely. Laura painted a picture of innocence, using Rachel's empathy to obscure the truth. Rachel's mind reeled as she pieced together the moments where she had been played, the subtle cues hidden in plain sight. The art, the ribbon, and the silent cries for help had all been part of a grander scheme.

Her hand trembled as she picked up a crimson ribbon, a beacon of Laura's fear, now a grotesque trophy of their shared deception. Rachel had been so blinded by her need to save Laura that she had ignored the signs of the artist's own dark heart. The ribbon slithered through her fingers like a blood-soaked snake, a chilling reminder of the depth of Laura's manipulation.

The walls in Laura's house were adorned with her art, each piece telling a twisted story of pain and control. Rachel had seen the fear and the pleas for help, but she had missed the malicious intent hidden beneath the strokes of Laura's brush. She had been the perfect audience, her traumatic past a mirror for Laura to reflect her twisted narrative. Rachel's stomach churned as she realized she had been a player in Laura's macabre theater, a prop to be used and discarded.

With a heavy heart, Rachel confronted Laura in the interrogation room, the crimson ribbon a stark reminder of the truth she had refused to see. Laura's eyes were cold; the gentle facade shattered like the glass from her paintings. Rachel had been so desperate to save Laura that she had ignored the monster lurking beneath the surface. "You painted your fear," Rachel said, her voice barely above a whisper. "But it was never just yours, was it?" Laura's smile was a chilling affirmation, a silent acknowledgment of Rachel's newfound understanding.

The artwork that once symbolized Laura's torment now hung in Rachel's mind like a series of twisted confessions. Each painting had been a step in their manipulation, a dance of shadows and lies that Rachel had been all too eager to follow. Laura had played Rachel like a fiddle; her strings pulled tight by the very emotion Rachel had thought she was there to save her from. Rachel felt the weight of her mistake, the lives lost because she had been too blinded by her need to believe in Laura's innocence.

"Why?" Rachel's voice was strained, the question a desperate plea for understanding. Laura's smile grew, a malicious twist of satisfaction that sent a shiver down Rachel's spine. "Why did you do this?" Rachel demanded, her voice echoing in the cold, sterile room. Laura leaned back in her chair, her eyes gleaming with a sick enjoyment of Rachel's turmoil.

"Because fear is power," Laura said, her voice low and smooth. I gave it to him, and he gave it back to me. It was a beautiful exchange." Rachel felt a chill run through her as she realized the depth of Laura's manipulation. Laura had used her fear, her pain, to control Mark and, by extension, Rachel. The crimson ribbon had been a silent language between them, a bond of horror that Rachel had unwittingly stepped into.

Rachel's hand clenched around the ribbon, her knuckles white. "But why me?" she asked, her voice barely above a whisper. Laura leaned forward, her eyes boring into Rachel's. "Because you were perfect," she said. "A detective with a heart of gold, a tragic past, a need to save the damsel in distress. You were my canvas, Rachel. You were the one who brought color to my art, who made it real." Rachel felt sick, the room spinning around her. Laura had painted her into this narrative, a character in her own twisted story.

<h1 style="text-align:center">Chapter 20</h1>

UNCOVERING THE TRUTH

"Your art," Rachel said, her voice trembling. "It's not about fear anymore, is it?" Laura's smile grew wider, her eyes gleaming with something that looked almost like admiration. "No," she said. "It's about power. And now, you're part of it." Rachel felt a coldness settle in her chest, realizing she had been a pawn in Laura's game all along. The art was a facade, a way to manipulate the emotions of those around her, to control the narrative, and to evade justice.

The silence in the room was palpable, the air thick with tension. Rachel's mind raced as she tried to process the horror of Laura's revelation. "You need to understand," Laura said, her voice soothing, almost seductive. "We're not so different, you and I. We both seek to control the chaos in our lives through art. But I've taken it to a new level, a masterpiece of fear and power." Rachel felt a wave of hate, the crimson ribbon in her hand now a noose tightening around her neck.

"It's over," Rachel said, her voice firm despite the turmoil. "You and Mark can't hurt anyone else." Laura's smile never wavered. "Is it, though?" she asked, tilting her head to the side. "Mark was only the beginning. You see, Rachel, fear is contagious. And with your help, I've learned to spread it like wildfire." Rachel's heart hammered in her chest, the gravity of Laura's words hitting her like a ton of bricks. Laura had been orchestrating this twisted dance all along, using Rachel's empathy as a conductor's baton to lead her through the symphony of terror.

The crimson ribbon lay on the table between them, a silent testament to Laura's manipulation. Rachel felt a wave of anger, her hand clenching into a fist around the ribbon. "You won't get away with this," Rachel said, her voice steady. Laura's eyes narrowed, the first crack in her facade. Rachel knew she had to keep pushing and find a way to dismantle the house of cards Laura had built.

"You think you're so clever," Rachel said, her tone laced with contempt. "Using your art to control, to play on people's fears. But it's over now. We have you both." Laura's smile was cold, unwavering. "You still don't understand," she said, her voice a purr. "Fear doesn't end with us. It's part of the world now, a part of everyone who's seen my work." Rachel's stomach twisted. Laura had twisted Rachel's empathy into a weapon, using her pain to fuel a cycle of fear and control.

"Your art," Rachel said, her voice tight. "It's not just about Mark's crimes anymore. It's about you. It's about what you've become." Laura leaned back, a smug expression on her face. "Fear is an artist's best muse," she said. "And I've painted with the crimson ribbon of terror for so long, it's become a part of me." Rachel felt a chill run down her spine. Laura had embraced the darkness, using her art to spread fear like a disease.

"But it ends here," Rachel said, her grip on the ribbon tightening. "You're going to pay for what you've done." Laura's smile grew, a twisted reflection of Rachel's determination. "You think you can contain fear?" she taunted. "It's in every brushstroke, every drop of paint. It's in the air we breathe, the shadows we cast." Rachel knew Laura was trying to get under her skin, to unravel the threads of her resolve. But Rachel was made of sterner stuff.

The book of Laura's life, the twisted story she had painted, was about to be closed. Rachel felt a surge of anger and determination. She had to be the one to bring Laura to justice, to ensure that her artful manipulation destroyed no more lives. "You're wrong," Rachel said, her voice cold. "Fear is a prison, and you'll be locked away." Laura's eyes widened, the first flicker of doubt crossing her face. Rachel could see the moment when Laura realized that she had underestimated her.

"Your art," Rachel continued, "It's not a masterpiece. It's a confession. And now, it's evidence." Rachel slammed her hand down on the table, the crimson ribbon fluttering like a bloody flag of victory. Laura's smile faltered, the cracks in her armor beginning to show. Rachel knew she had to keep pressing and shatter the illusion Laura had so carefully constructed.

"You can't hide behind your paintings anymore," Rachel said, her voice like steel. "We're going to dissect every piece, every stroke, and we're going to lay bare the truth." Laura's eyes narrowed a flicker of anger in the depths of her soul. Rachel could see the cogs turning, the wheels of Laura's mind searching for an escape. But Rachel was ready for her; her resolve was as unyielding as the ribbon she held.

"You think you know me?" Laura spat, her voice laced with venom. "You've only seen what I've allowed you to see. You're just a detective playing art critic, trying to solve a puzzle with no solution." Rachel's grip on the ribbon tightened. "No," she said firmly. "I'm a detective who will bring you to justice." Laura's smile was cold, her eyes hard. "You're a fool," she said. "You've been dancing in my web the whole time."

The interrogation room walls seemed to close in, the air thick with the stench of Laura's arrogance. Rachel knew she had to keep her calm and outsmart the woman who had played her so expertly. "Your art is your downfall," Rachel said, her voice a knife. "It's going to be the noose that hangs you." Laura's smile didn't falter. "You think you can use my art against me?" she asked mockingly. "It's already part of you, Rachel. You can't escape it."

But Rachel had an ace up her sleeve. She studied Laura's art and saw the patterns and signs of her madness woven into every piece. "Your art is a map to your soul," Rachel said, her voice low and intense. "And it will lead us to everyone you've hurt." Laura's eyes narrowed, the faintest trace of worry flickering in her gaze. Rachel leaned in, her voice a whisper. "We're going to dissect every painting and brushstroke until we uncover every lie."

Laura's smile was brittle, a mask cracking under Rachel's relentless stare. Rachel knew she had her, knew that the walls of Laura's twisted reality were starting to crumble. "You're wrong," Laura said, but her voice wavered. Rachel could see the doubt creeping in, the fear of being exposed. "No," Rachel said, her voice firm. "I'm not. Your art is your confession, and it will be the key to your cage." Laura's eyes darted around the room, searching for an escape, but Rachel had her cornered.

The crimson ribbon lay on the table between them, a silent witness to Laura's manipulation. Rachel picked it up, feeling the weight of its history in her hand. "This ribbon," Rachel said, her voice steady. "It's not just a symbol of fear anymore. It's a symbol of your power, your control. And now, the rope will tie you to your crimes." Laura's eyes narrowed, and Rachel could see the wheels turning in her mind. Laura was trying to find a way out to twist the narrative back in her favor.

But Rachel was ready for her. "Your art," Rachel continued, her voice like a scalpel slicing through the lies. "It's a blueprint of your soul, a road map to the truth." Laura's smug expression began to crumble, her eyes darting around the room as Rachel's words hit home. Rachel leaned in, her gaze unwavering. "Every brushstroke, every drop of paint tells a story. And we'll read it, line by line, until we reach the end." Laura's breath grew shallow, the first signs of panic flitting across her face. Rachel knew she had to keep the pressure on.

"We're going to dissect your art, Laura," Rachel said, her voice cold and steady. "We're going to pull it apart until we find every thread of manipulation and hint of your true intentions." Laura's eyes widened, the crimson ribbon seeming to pulse with an evil energy. Rachel could almost hear the whirl of thoughts racing through Laura's mind, searching for a way to regain control. But Rachel had the upper hand, her empathy sharpened into a weapon.

Chapter 21

THE SHOCKING CONFESSION

"We're going to dissect your art, Laura," Rachel said, her voice cold and steady. "We're going to pull it apart until we find every thread of manipulation and hint of your true intentions." Laura's eyes widened, the crimson ribbon seeming to pulse with an evil energy. Rachel could almost hear the whirl of thoughts racing through Laura's mind, searching for a way to regain control. But Rachel had the upper hand, her empathy sharpened into a weapon.

"You think you're so clever," Laura spat, her calm facade slipping. "But you're just a pawn in my game." Rachel leaned back in her chair, the crimson ribbon clutched tightly in her hand. "Your art won't save you now," she said. "It's going to be the noose that tightens around your neck." Laura's smile grew brittle, the cracks in her confidence widening. Rachel knew she had struck a nerve.

The silence between them was tense, the air charged with Laura's desperation. Rachel could almost see the gears turning in Laura's mind, searching for a way to escape the prison she had built with her brush. "Make a deal," Laura said, voice low and urgent. "I can give you Mark.

I can make him confess to everything." Rachel raised an eyebrow, intrigued despite herself.

"What do you want?" Rachel asked, her tone wary. Laura leaned forward, her eyes gleaming with a cunning that sent a chill down Rachel's spine. "Immunity," Laura said. "For me and my art. I'll tell you everything, but you must promise to protect my work. It's not just about Mark anymore." Rachel felt a flicker of doubt, the crimson ribbon in her hand a stark reminder of Laura's manipulation. But the opportunity to end the horror was too tempting to resist.

"Fine," Rachel said, her voice tight. "You give us Mark and the truth, and we'll consider it." Laura's smile grew, a twisted victory in her eyes. Rachel knew she had to tread carefully; Laura was still a master of the game, even in defeat. "Good," Laura said, leaning back in her chair. "Now, let's talk about the real artistry here." Rachel's stomach turned as Laura began to lay out her twisted plan, her words painting a picture of a world where fear and manipulation were the ultimate forms of power.

As Laura spoke, Rachel couldn't help but think of the crimson ribbon, now a symbol of the tangled web of deceit that had trapped her. It had been a tool of fear in Laura's hands, a silent scream in the canvas of her life. But now, it was Rachel's turn to wield it, to unravel the dark tapestry Laura had woven. Rachel's mind raced, trying to piece together the puzzle of Laura's words to find the truth hidden beneath the layers of lies.

"It started when I was young," Laura began, her voice eerily calm. "I discovered that fear could be shaped, molded into something beautiful. Something powerful. And when I met Mark, I saw in him the perfect canvas for my art." Rachel felt a chill as Laura spoke of her twisted beginnings; the sickness in her soul laid bare. Laura had found in Mark a kindred spirit, a man whose depravity matched her own. Together, they had painted a picture of horror that had claimed so many lives.

"He was lost," Laura continued, her eyes distant. "He had the capacity for fear but no direction. I showed him how to harness it and make it into something more. And with the crimson ribbon, I gave him a signature, a symbol of our partnership." Rachel's mind reeled as she listened to Laura's account; the ribbon now symbolized their twisted union. Laura had found Mark, not as a victim, but as an accomplice, a means to an end.

"I saw the fear in him," Laura said, her voice almost wistful. "The way it consumed him, the way it made him weak. I knew I could mold him, use him to bring my art to life." Rachel felt her stomach twist as Laura described the manipulation with a sense of pride, her art a canvas for the fear she had taught Mark to wield. Once a symbol of Laura's fear, the ribbon had become a tool of power, a crimson thread connecting them in a dance of terror.

"We met at an exhibition," Laura continued, her eyes glinting with the memory. "He was lost, overwhelmed by the darkness within. He didn't know how to harness it or make it beautiful." Laura had found Mark, a man whose fears mirrored her own, and had taught him to embrace them, to use them as a weapon. The art they had created together was not a cry for help but a declaration of war on the unsuspecting world.

"He was like a wild beast," Laura said, her voice taking on a dreamy quality. "I saw his potential, the raw power just waiting to be unleashed. I taught him how to focus his fear, to make it into something tangible. And with the crimson ribbon, I gave him a purpose." Rachel felt a chill as Laura spoke of her twisted mentorship, her art a means to cultivate Mark's depravity. The ribbon, once a symbol of Laura's fear, had become a leash, guiding Mark through a nightmare landscape of their own making.

"Together, we became more than the sum of our parts," Laura

continued, her eyes shining with a manic light. "We created something beautiful, something that made people feel alive. The ribbon was our signature, a crimson thread woven through every act of terror." Rachel could see the delusion in Laura's eyes, how she had convinced herself that their partnership was a work of art rather than a catalog of suffering. But Rachel knew the truth, knew that Laura's art was not a masterpiece but a manifesto of madness.

"How many, Laura?" Rachel asked, her voice hard. "How many people did you and Mark terrorize with your art?" Laura's smile was cold, her eyes calculating. "As many as the brushstrokes in my paintings," she said. Rachel felt a wave of anger and disgust wash over her. Laura had a number; of course, she did. Each victim was a stroke on her canvas, a note in her symphony of fear. Rachel knew she had to keep pushing and get Laura to confess.

"We're going to find them all," Rachel said, her voice like ice. "Every person you've hurt, every family you've destroyed." Laura's smile grew, a twisted mockery of Rachel's determination. "You think you can quantify fear?" she asked. "It's not about the numbers, Rachel. It's about the impact. The way it changes people, the way it makes them feel alive." Rachel's hand tightened around the crimson ribbon, her knuckles white. Laura's words were a challenge, a dare to prove her wrong.

Chapter 22

T HE PURSUIT ENDS

Just then, Sam's voice crackled over the intercom. "Rachel, we need you in the observation room." Rachel felt annoyed at the interruption but knew she had to trust her partner. She stood, the crimson ribbon still clutched in her hand and walked out of the interrogation room. Laura's laughter followed her, a haunting echo in the sterile corridor. Rachel took a deep breath, trying to shake off the feeling of Laura's words clinging to her like a cobweb.

In the observation room, Sam handed Rachel a box, the contents of which made her heart sink. Inside, neatly typed on a stack of papers, were the names of all the victims they had linked to Laura and Mark's reign of terror. Rachel's eyes scanned the list, her heart heavy with the weight of each name. "Forensics found this at Laura's house," Sam said, his voice grim. "It's over," Rachel murmured, her voice hollow. "It's all here."

The crimson ribbon in Rachel's pocket felt like a brand, a constant reminder of Laura's manipulation. Rachel knew that the battle was far from over; they had to bring closure to the victims' families and ensure

Laura's art of fear didn't inspire more like her. Rachel's mind raced, piecing the puzzle of Laura's confession with the cold, hard evidence in her hand. Laura had painted a dreadful picture of her life's work, and Rachel was now holding the key to dismantling it.

Sam's eyes met Rachel's, mirroring her horror. They had caught a glimpse of the monster they had been hunting, and now they could unmask it completely. Rachel took the box, her hand trembling slightly. Each name represented a life stolen, a family left to grapple with the shadow of Laura's art. The list was a grim reminder of the depth of Laura's obsession, a tangible connection to the people whose fears had been her canvas.

"Read her her rights," Rachel instructed Sam, her voice firm despite the turmoil. She couldn't bear to be in the same room with Laura anymore, not with the truth before her. Rachel turned and walked away, her footsteps echoing down the hallway, leaving Laura's taunts behind her. The crimson ribbon felt like a lead weight in her pocket, a constant pulse of anger and disgust that matched the rhythm of her heart.

As Rachel stepped out into the cool night air, she felt the weight of the case pressing down on her. Laura's art had been a prison for so many, a labyrinth of fear and manipulation that Rachel had been forced to navigate. She took a deep breath, the chilly breeze carrying the distant sounds of the city, a stark contrast to the stifling confines of the interrogation room.

Her mind was a whirlwind of thoughts and emotions, each victim's name a flaming torch in the darkness of Laura's twisted gallery. Rachel knew that before facing the families, she needed to find some semblance of peace to shake off the cobwebs of Laura's deceit. She climbed into her car, the leather seats cold against her skin, and drove home with a heavy heart.

Once inside her apartment, Rachel tossed the crimson ribbon onto the kitchen counter, its stark color contrasting with the soft light of her living room. She poured herself a stiff drink, the amber liquid glinting in the glass like a warning of the turmoil ahead. Rachel knew that the ribbon would be a constant reminder of the case, of the lives destroyed by Laura's art, but she couldn't bring herself to touch it again that night.

Her mind racing, Rachel tried to organize her thoughts. Each name on the list was a story waiting to be told, a family desperate for answers. She had to find a way to give them closure, to somehow mend the holes Laura had torn in their lives. Rachel took a long sip of her drink, the burn of the alcohol a temporary salve for the pain that Laura had inflicted on her and so many others.

With a sigh, Rachel made her way to her bedroom, the walls adorned with her art, starkly contrasting with Laura's crimson chaos. She stripped off her clothes, the fabric clinging to her like the memories of Laura's words. As she slipped into bed, Rachel couldn't shake the feeling that Laura was still watching her, that the crimson ribbon was a direct line to the artist's soul. She pulled the covers over her head, willing herself to find peace in the darkness.

Chapter 23

T HE AFTERMATH

The following day, Rachel and Sam assembled a team of officers to begin the grim task of locating the bodies of Laura and Mark's victims. The list in Rachel's hand was a map of pain, each name a location to be marked with a crimson ribbon as a grim reminder of their mission. The foggy marina was their first stop, the water lapping against the dock like a whispered taunt. Rachel's eyes searched the murky depths, haunted by the memory of Mark's escape and Laura's cold gaze.

The dive team descended into the water, their lights cutting through the gloom like the truth slicing through Laura's lies. Rachel watched from the boat, her mind racing with images of the art that had led them here. The crimson ribbon felt like a brand on her conscience, symbolizing the fear she had underestimated. As the hours ticked by, the tension grew tauter than a bowstring. Each splash of water, each glimpse of a shadow, sent Rachel's heart racing.

Finally, a hand surfaced, clutching a soggy piece of fabric. Rachel's stomach lurched as they pulled a ribbon-wrapped skeletal hand into view. The ribbon, once a vibrant crimson, had faded to a dull maroon, stained by the murky waters of the marina. Laura's art had claimed so many lives, leaving behind a macabre still life in the depths. Rachel felt a mix of anger and sorrow, her determination to bring justice to the victims growing stronger with each grim discovery.

The dive team worked tirelessly, their grim task a silent ballet of recovery and respect. Each body was brought to the surface carefully, the crimson ribbon contrasting with the cold, lifeless skin. Rachel stood on the boat, her eyes never leaving the water, her mind racing with the faces of the people whose fears Laura had used as her canvas. With each recovery, Rachel whispered a silent apology, a promise that their suffering would not be forgotten.

The marina grew quiet as the day wore on; the only sounds were the splash of the divers and the occasional cry of a seagull piercing the air. Rachel's eyes burned with anger and sorrow, her heart heavy with the lives lost to Laura's twisted artistry. The crimson ribbon symbolized the fear they had all underestimated, a crimson thread connecting the living to the dead.

One by one, the divers emerged from the water, each bringing a grim trophy of Laura's game. Rachel felt a part of her die with every rib-boned corpse that was lifted onto the boat. Each one was a story untold, a life snuffed out by the brushstroke of Laura's madness. Rachel knew she had to stay strong, to be the voice for those who no longer had one.

The forensic team worked meticulously, treating each body with the dignity it deserved. Rachel watched as they cataloged each ribbon, a silent scream of color against the monochrome of death. The crimson hue had faded, but its power remained, a stark reminder of the fear Laura had so expertly wielded. Rachel's mind was tumultuous—grief, anger, and a burning need for justice.

As the bodies were carefully placed into body bags, Rachel couldn't help but think of the lives that Laura's twisted vision had snuffed out. Each ribbon declared war on innocence, a crimson scar on the fabric of the city's soul. She felt the weight of each life lost, a heavy burden she bore as a detective sworn to protect and serve.

The search at the marina continued into the night, the fog thickening like a shroud around them. The water was a cold, unforgiving witness to Laura and Mark's crimes, giving up its secrets individually. Rachel's eyes never left the surface, searching for the next clue, the following body that would bring them closer to understanding the extent of their depravity.

Each time a ribboned hand emerged from the depths, Rachel felt a new wave of nausea wash over her. The water swallowed the crimson color, leaving behind a ghostly pallor that spoke of the decay beneath. Laura's art had become a horrible reality, each ribbon a twisted reminder of her obsession with fear. Rachel's thoughts turned to the families who would soon receive the devastating news, their lives forever altered by the crimson ribbon.

The boat's engine hummed mournfully as they approached the following location, the fog thickening like a living entity that didn't want them to find the truth. Rachel's hand clenched around the list, her knuckles white. Each name represented a battle lost, a soul claimed by Laura's insatiable hunger for power. As the divers disappeared beneath the surface again, Rachel whispered a silent prayer for their strength and guidance.

The first glimpse of a new crimson ribbon sent a shockwave through Rachel's body. It was tied around a young woman's wrist, her eyes open wide in a silent scream, forever captured in Laura's twisted art. Rachel's eyes filled with tears as the divers brought her up, her heart aching for the families who would soon learn the terrible fate of their loved ones. The ribbon had once symbolized Laura's fear, but now it was a grim signature of her control.

Chapter 24

JUSTICE FOR THE VICTIMS

Two days later, the list was complete, and all the bodies had been discovered. Rachel sat in her office, the walls covered in photos and notes from the case, her eyes red and swollen from lack of sleep. The crimson ribbon lay on her desk, a silent accusation of her failure to see through Laura's manipulation sooner. Each time Rachel looked at it, she felt anger, pity, and a strange kinship with Laura's victims.

The final count was higher than anticipated, a grim testament to Laura and Mark's twisted artistry. Rachel had read through each file, memorizing the names and faces of those lost to the crimson ribbon's grip. She had promised herself she would not rest until Laura faced the full extent of her crimes.

The press had picked up on the story, and the crimson ribbon had become a city-wide symbol of fear and tragedy. Rachel knew she had to be careful with her words to ensure Laura's art didn't claim more victims through sensationalism. She stepped in front of the podium, the ribbon pinned to her lapel like a declaration of war. "We have found all the known victims of Laura Davis and Mark Castellanos's crimes," she announced, her voice steady despite the tremor in her heart. "Our priority now is to bring their families closure and to ensure that Laura is brought to justice for her heinous acts."

The flashbulbs popped like a thousand silent screams; the reporters' faces were a blur of white light and hungry curiosity. Rachel's gaze remained unflinching, her eyes a steely blue that matched the ribbon's crimson. She had to be the beacon of hope in this darkness, the voice that promised retribution. "The crimson ribbon," she continued, "once a symbol of fear, will now symbolize our resilience. We will not let Laura Davis's art define us. We will not let fear win."

The room was a cacophony of questions, each piercing Rachel's resolve like a knife. But she had a plan, a way to twist Laura's art back into something beautiful—justice. Rachel turned to Sam, who nodded solemnly. They had worked tirelessly, tracing the ribbon's crimson path through the city's underbelly, uncovering the sickening reality behind each brushstroke. It was time to confront Laura with the truth she had painted in blood.

The prison walls felt colder than usual as Rachel and Sam entered the visitation room. Laura sat across the table, her eyes gleaming with anticipation and amusement. Rachel laid out the evidence, each piece a stroke of crimson defiance against Laura's art of fear. The artist's smile faltered, the first crack in her façade. "You think you can cage me with your truth?" Laura hissed her voice a serpent's whisper. Rachel leaned in, her voice a low, determined growl. "I'm not here to cage you. I'm here to show you the consequences of your art."

The crimson ribbon on Rachel's lapel fluttered with each word, a silent accusation that Laura couldn't ignore. Rachel laid out the list of names, each a stark reminder of the lives she had destroyed. Laura's eyes darted to the ribbon, then back to Rachel, her expression unreadable. "These people," Rachel said, her voice heavy with emotion, "weren't just your subjects. They were daughters, sons, fathers, and friends. They had lives, dreams, and fears. You used those fears to create your twisted masterpieces."

Laura's smile grew thinner, a brittle veneer over her rage. "Masterpieces," she spat. "You think you can understand art?" Rachel slammed her hand on the table, the ribbon snapping against her chest. "This isn't art, Laura. This is murder. You didn't just manipulate fear; you bathed in it. You painted with the blood of the innocent." Laura's eyes narrowed, her grip tightening around the table's edge. "You don't know what it's like," she whispered. "The power of fear, the beauty of it. It's intoxicating."

Rachel leaned closer, her eyes boring into Laura's. "And now," she said, her voice low and deadly, "you're going to watch as we dismantle your canvas, piece by piece. You're going to face every single person you hurt. You're going to hear their stories, their fears, their pain. And you're going to realize that your art isn't power. It's just a prison, and now it's your turn to be trapped inside it." Laura's eyes flashed like panic, and Rachel knew she had hit a nerve.

Chapter 25

THE TRIAL

The trial was a spectacle, a macabre exhibition of Laura's crimes. Rachel sat in the courtroom, the crimson ribbon wrapped around her wrist like a silent sentinel. Laura's art was displayed on the walls, each testament to her depravity. The jurors gasped as the evidence was presented, the crimson ribbon weaving a chilling narrative through the lives of her victims. Rachel watched Laura closely, looking for any sign of remorse, any crack in the façade of the artist who had painted with fear. But Laura's expression remained calm, almost serene, as if admiring her twisted gallery.

The prosecutor laid out the details of each crime, the crimson ribbon a grim thread connecting the dots of Laura's madness. Rachel's stomach turned as the autopsy reports were read aloud, the ribbon a silent rebuke to Laura's claim of artistic expression. Yet Laura's gaze never wavered, her eyes gleaming with a cold, detached amusement. It was as if she were watching a play she had written, her macabre production coming to life before her eyes.

As the days of the trial dragged on, Rachel felt the weight of the ribbon on her wrist grow heavier. The victims' families filled the benches, their faces a tapestry of grief and anger. Rachel knew she had to be the one to ensure Laura's art was recognized for what it indeed was: a canvas of fear and manipulation, not a masterpiece. The ribbon symbolized the power Laura had held over her and Mark, a tool that had allowed them to weave their terrible tapestry of fear.

During the trial's final moments, Rachel took the stand, her voice steady and unwavering. She spoke of the nights spent unraveling Laura's twisted narrative and the moments she had felt the artist's influence tighten around her mind. The jury watched her intently, their faces a mirror of the horror Rachel had thought in the depths of Laura's world. Rachel held up the crimson ribbon, now faded and stained with the grime of the marina. "This is not art," she said, her voice resonating through the silent courtroom. "This is the tool of a monster." Laura's smile faltered, the first real emotion Rachel had seen from her since the chase ended with Mark's plunge into the water.

The defense tried to paint Laura as a tortured soul, a misunderstood genius whose art had been misinterpreted. Rachel watched, her eyes never leaving Laura's, as the lawyer spoke of her crimson ribbon ritual's "beauty" in fear and the "therapeutic" nature. Rachel felt a surge of anger, her hand clenching around the ribbon. But she knew better than to let it show, to give Laura the satisfaction of knowing she had gotten under her skin. Instead, Rachel waited, her mind racing with the counterarguments she knew would come.

The prosecutor returned her to the stand, and Rachel faced Laura again. The artist's eyes searched hers, looking for a crack in her resolve. Rachel took a deep breath and dismantled Laura's narrative piece by piece, using the ribbon as a visual aid. She explained how Laura had manipulated Mark and how she had used her art to control and dominate. The jury watched, transfixed, as Rachel unraveled the twisted logic behind each crimson thread.

Laura's smile grew strained as Rachel spoke, her eyes darting around the room. Rachel could see the doubt creeping in, the realization that her artful manipulation was being dissected and displayed for all to see. The ribbon had become a noose, tightening around Laura's neck with each word Rachel uttered. The detective's voice grew stronger, each syllable a blow to Laura's carefully constructed reality.

The prosecutor rested his case, and the defense began their plea. Rachel watched as Laura's lawyer painted a picture of a troubled artist, misunderstood by a society that feared her brilliance. Rachel's knuckles turned white as she gripped the crimson ribbon, a silent rebuttal to the lies being spun. Laura's gaze never left Rachel, a silent challenge that Rachel met with a steely resolve.

As the defense droned on, Rachel felt the tension in the courtroom thickens. She knew the jury was wavering, torn between the horror of Laura's crimes and the seductive allure of her art. Rachel had to act fast. She approached the prosecutor, her voice low and urgent. "We need to do something," she whispered. "We can't let her win."

The prosecutor nodded gravely, and Rachel took the stand once more. She held up the crimson ribbon, its once-vibrant color now a sad, faded echo of its former power. "This," she said, her voice clear and strong, "is not the mark of a misunderstood genius. This is the signature of a woman who used fear as her canvas and the lives of others as her paint." Rachel's words hung in the air, contrasting Laura's artful defense.

The defense attorney's eyes narrowed, sensing Rachel's newfound confidence. Rachel met Laura's gaze, her eyes no longer haunted by the crimson ribbon's sway but instead filled with the resolve to bring her to justice. She continued, her voice growing stronger with each syllable. "Your honor, Laura Davis didn't just manipulate Mark; she manipulated us all. She painted a picture of fear so convincing that we became part of her twisted reality. But fear does not make art. It makes monsters."

The judge banged his gavel, signaling the end of the trial. The room remained still, the only sound of the rustle of papers and the quiet sobs of the victims' families. Rachel stepped down from the stand, her eyes never leaving Laura's. The artist's smug expression had been replaced by something else—fear. Rachel felt a strange mix of satisfaction and sadness. Laura had been unmasked, but at what cost?

The jury deliberated for what felt like an eternity, the ribbon a constant reminder of the lives lost and the truth Rachel had sworn to reveal. Rachel paced outside the courtroom, the crimson ribbon wrapped tightly around her wrist like a brand. Sam placed a comforting hand on her shoulder, but Rachel barely noticed. Her mind was racing with the details of the case, the faces of the victims, and the chilling confessions Laura had made.

Finally, the doors creaked open, and the jury's foreman announced their verdict. Rachel's heart pounded as she heard the words she had hoped for but never truly allowed herself to believe. "Guilty on all counts." Laura's eyes widened, the color draining from her face as the reality of her fate set in. Rachel felt a weight lift from her shoulders, but it was quickly replaced by a new burden—ensuring that Laura's manipulation would not continue to haunt her from behind bars.

The courtroom erupted into chaos, the crimson ribbon fluttering in Rachel's hand as she passed through the sea of reporters and spectators. She could hear Laura's cries of protest and the desperate clanging of the handcuffs as she was escorted out. Rachel stepped outside into the cool evening air; the ribbon now symbolized victory rather than fear. The city lights reflected off the damp pavement, starkly contrasting the darkness Laura had brought into the world.

As Rachel walked towards her car, the weight of the verdict finally settled upon her. The crimson ribbon had been the key to Laura's downfall, a twisted tool of manipulation that Rachel had wielded with precision. The case had taken a toll on her, but the conviction was a beacon of hope in the otherwise grim landscape of her thoughts. Rachel felt a sense of relief but also a profound sadness for the lives lost, and the families left behind.

The media frenzy grew as Rachel approached the parking lot, and the flashes of cameras and the cacophony of questions were a stark reminder of the public's hunger for closure. Rachel held the ribbon tightly, using it as a shield against the barrage of curiosity. The symbol that once haunted her now stood for justice, starkly contrasting the fear it had once invoked. With Sam by her side, Rachel navigated through the chaos, her eyes fixed on the horizon where the dark clouds of the case were slowly beginning to dissipate.

Once in the quiet solitude of her car, Rachel allowed herself to breathe deeply, the weight of the ribbon's significance pressing into her palm. The trial had ended, but the battle was far from over. Laura was just one player in a giant game of manipulation and fear. Rachel knew that the crimson ribbon would forever be a part of her, a scarlet reminder of the depths of human depravity and the importance of her role in bringing those responsible to justice. She looked at the ribbon, feeling the power it had once held over her dissipate. It symbolized her triumph, a declaration that fear could be conquered.

Chapter 26

CONCLUSION

The drive back to the precinct was a blur, Rachel's thoughts racing as she contemplated the journey ahead. Laura's art would be studied, dissected, and ultimately forgotten, but her destroyed lives would never be restored. Rachel's eyes filled with tears as she thought of the victims' families, the anguish they had endured, and the long road to healing that lay before them. The crimson ribbon was a testament to their pain, a silent promise that she would not rest until all those responsible were brought to justice.

As Rachel and Sam entered the station, the atmosphere was electric. Colleagues offered congratulations and slap on the back, but Rachel felt only the solemn weight of her victory. The ribbon was now a symbol of the darkness she had faced and the strength she had found to conquer it. She knew that the case was not just about Laura and Mark but about the many other unseen players in the shadowy world of fear and manipulation. Rachel's commitment to the truth had dismantled Laura's empire and shone a light on the city's hidden corners where fear lurked.

The detective sat at her desk, the ribbon coiled like a sleeping snake. She knew the fight against fear would be a lifelong battle, but she had tasted victory, which only made her more determined. Rachel pulled out her notepad and scribbled down the next steps in her quest for justice. There were more criminals to catch and more lives to save. The art of fear was not exclusive to Laura; it was a tool used by many, and Rachel was now its unyielding adversary.

The precinct buzzed with renewed energy as Rachel's success spread through the ranks. Detectives approached her with newfound respect, eager to share their unsolved cases, hoping she could see the unseen patterns. Rachel listened intently, her mind already racing ahead, connecting the dots that only she could see. Her journey from manipulated pawn to empowered adversary had just begun.

In the quiet of her office, Rachel placed the crimson ribbon in a clear evidence bag, sealing it with a quiet finality. It was no longer a symbol of fear but a trophy of justice. Her eyes fell upon the photos of the victims pinned to the corkboard, their smiles frozen in time. Rachel knew that she had not just fought for their justice; she had also fought for the countless others who had suffered under Laura's reign of terror.

The case had taken a toll on Rachel, leaving her with scars that no ribbon could cover. Yet, as she stared at the wall of evidence, she felt a surge of determination. Laura was just the beginning. Rachel knew there were more monsters like her out there, weaving their crimson threads through the fabric of society. It was her duty to snip those threads until the tapestry of fear was nothing but a fading memory.

THE END

www.ingramcontent.com/pod-product-compliance
Lightning Source LLC
Chambersburg PA
CBHW071336140726
47996CB00005B/2004